The Four Children of Night

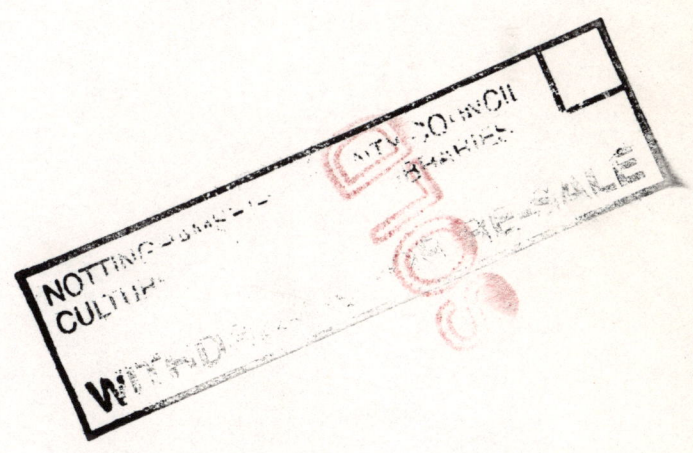

Other books by Weem Whitaker

Seeking the Worm
The Bold Enchanter

The Four Children of Night

Weem Whitaker

OXFORD
UNIVERSITY PRESS

Great Clarendon Street, Oxford OX2 6DP
Oxford University Press is a department of the University of Oxford.
It furthers the University's objective of excellence in research, scholarship,
and education by publishing worldwide in

Oxford New York

Athens Auckland Bangkok Bogotá Buenos Aires Calcutta
Cape Town Chennai Dar es Salaam Delhi Florence Hong Kong Istanbul
Karachi Kuala Lumpur Madrid Melbourne Mexico City Mumbai
Nairobi Paris São Paulo Singapore Taipei Tokyo Toronto Warsaw
and associated companies in Berlin Ibadan

Oxford is a registered trade mark of Oxford University Press
in the UK and in certain other countries

Copyright © Weem Whitaker 2000

The moral rights of the author have been asserted

First published 2000

1 3 5 7 9 10 8 6 4 2

All rights reserved. No part of this publication may be reproduced,
stored in a retrieval system, or transmitted, in any form or by any means,
without the prior permission in writing of Oxford University Press.
Within the UK, exceptions are allowed in respect of any fair
dealing for the purpose of research or private study, or criticism or
review, as permitted under the Copyright, Designs and Patents Act 1988,
or in the case of reprographic reproduction in accordance with
the terms of the licences issued by the Copyright Licensing Agency.
Enquiries concerning reproduction outside these terms and in other
countries should be sent to the Rights Department, Oxford University Press,
at the above address.

This book is sold subject to the condition that it shall not, by way of trade or
otherwise, be lent, re-sold, hired out or otherwise circulated without
the publisher's prior consent in any form of binding or cover other than that in
which it is published and without a similar condition including this condition
being imposed on the subsequent purchaser.

British Library Cataloguing in Publication Data available

ISBN 0 19 271846 0

Typeset by AFS Image Setters Ltd, Glasgow
Printed and bound in Great Britain by
Biddles Ltd, Guildford and King's Lynn

Nottinghamshire County Council
Community Services

For Katie

Contents

1	The Storms	1
2	The Cave of Holla	11
3	Land Without End	19
4	Fire and Hail	26
5	Lord of Storms	36
6	Stargazers and Telkins	41
7	The Labyrinth	52
8	War Below Ground	60
9	Birchbark and Chimneysoot	65
10	The Book of Endings	72
11	Plans by Firelight	79
12	Travels without a Map	82
13	The Top of the World	88
14	The Mother of All	95
15	Truth	100
16	The Last Book	106

1
The Storms

Peter was sitting by the fire while the wind howled round the house. It snatched at the eaves and sent smoke eddying back down the chimney, making him cough. And over the sound of the wind he could always hear the waves crashing not far off, down on the shore where the fishing boats were kept. Peter was worried. He knew he shouldn't be: there've been storms before, he told himself, storms just as wild and fierce as this one, which went on for days just the same. They'd pulled the boat up well above the reach of the sea, so what could there be to worry about? But he couldn't comfort himself. He still felt something was wrong.

The others didn't seem to feel it. His father went on mending his nets by the fire, his pipe in his mouth, and when the roof creaked or the fire smoked he would just cock his eye up at the storm quizzically, as if it were getting a bit above itself. Peter's two younger sisters weren't troubled either. Lotta, the youngest, thought the storm was exciting. And Kari wanted to play.

'What at?' Peter asked her, abstracted.

'Shipwrecks and storms,' Kari replied. 'I'll stand on the stool and you be the sea and wash me off, and then we all get *drowned*.'

Peter's worry snapped into anger. 'You're not to play about it!' he shouted. 'This is real! Can't you hear the wind? There's *danger*!'

Lotta, who had been staring at them hoping there'd be a way for her to join in the game, began to cry. Their mother turned from her cooking.

'Peter!' she scolded. 'You're not to frighten Lotta. It's only a storm, like we've often had. It'll pass. They always do.' She bent down to comfort Lotta, and Peter felt miserable. His mother looked up at him. 'What's the matter with you?'

But Peter didn't know. That night he lay awake while the others slept, listening to the sound of the storm. The wind wailed round the roof, then whined off through the stiff sea-grass or rattled among the salted fish hanging outside on their wooden racks to dry, while the sea crashed and roared down on the shore. He thought the wind and the waves had never sounded so wildly driven, so full of feeling and life, and he was frightened. The only time he'd felt like this before was once when Kari had dared him to step inside the Shipstones. He'd gone quite close—closer than he'd been before; he'd almost passed between two of the sombre, looming stones and stepped inside the ring. But then a feeling of such dread had come over him that he'd turned and run. Kari had been surprised—too surprised to laugh.

He turned over restlessly. He couldn't believe he was being so foolish. Even Lotta, who was five, wasn't afraid. It was only a storm. He tried to remember the last one they'd had; the wind must have wailed and the waves must have crashed in exactly the same way. So what was different? He lay fretting and puzzling, one moment sure and the next in doubt, and slipped into uneasy sleep.

The gale blew all night, but next day the wind slackened. Towards evening a weak sun broke through a tear in the clouds for the first time in seven days, bringing colour back to a world that seemed to Peter to have been grey forever.

'Is it over?' Kari shouted. 'Can we go out? Are you going to fish?'

Peter's father peered past them at the sea, and gave a satisfied nod. 'It's over, all right. The wind's dropped right down. Sea's still a bit troubled, but nothing to worry us. We're in luck. It'll be fresh fish for us, tonight.'

Peter felt a sudden stab of foreboding. 'You're not going to take the boat out?'

His father turned to him. 'Why not?'

'I mean—' Peter stopped. It was so hard to explain what he felt—the sense of menace, of something still not being right in the sound of the wind and the sea. 'I mean,' he began again, 'why don't I go up to the hilltop, and see if it's really all right?'

His father gave him a smile, puzzled. 'Off you go if you want to, then. But be sure you're back soon, and help me run the boat down the beach.'

Peter sped off. Kari and Lotta were already out of the door, and Kari was beginning on one of her dangerous games, walking along the keel of an upturned fishing boat.

'Come on!' she shouted to him. 'See if you can do what I can do!'

But Peter didn't stop. 'Don't go far!' he called back. 'And keep an eye on Lotta!'

He ran on, out through the village and up the heathery slope to the place he called the Hill. As he ran he listened. The low whisper of the wind and the dull sigh of the waves troubled him almost more than the storm had; it was as if the sea were nursing some secret anger.

A few minutes later he stood breathless on the very highest point of the island. He could see everything from up here. His whole world lay around him: the Island, the only land he'd ever known, and the wide sea beyond. Right below him was the village. It still looked close, and

Peter found himself thinking he could reach it in a hurry if he had to.

But why? Why was he so worried? The clouds were clearing quickly, moving off east towards the Mainland, a distant blur on the horizon; and to the west, where the storms always came from, the sun was setting in a calm, golden sky. I ought to go back, Peter thought, tell them it's safe and help father take the boat out . . .

But still there was the strange sound of the sea. Long, uneasy waves heaved themselves up and washed over the rocks down on the shore, then pulled themselves back with a groan. There was something in the sound that really was like a voice, murmuring and lilting, complaining, perhaps, or lamenting. Straining to hear more clearly, he began to walk down the slope towards the seaward side of the Island.

It was wild here, and windswept. There were no houses, and no trees: only the rugged black shapes of the Shipstones, right ahead of him. There were twelve of them, curving up from the heather in a double rank like the ribs of a ship, with stout stone pillars at either end for the stem and the stern. The villagers rarely came to this side of the Island, and they kept well clear of the Shipstones.

Hardly aware that he was doing it, Peter now made a wide swing to the left, avoiding the Shipstones, still drawn on down to the sea. Right above the rocks lining the shore he stopped. He was surer than ever now that the sea had a voice. When the waves came in it mounted like a dirge, and as the sea broke on the rocks the sadness of it surged all round him and seemed to tug at him, down towards the water.

'The sea's not angry,' Peter murmured. 'It's sad. It's suffering—crying for help.'

And there are words, he thought. For a moment he

could almost hear them; they lingered on the edge of his hearing, just out of reach, then slipped away and were lost. He moved forward again, listening, hoping that somehow the sense of the song would remain long enough for him to grasp it; but after a few steps he stopped with a shock.

He had come too far. Right in front of him were the Seafolk, crowds and crowds of them, standing quite still with their backs to him, staring out over the sea. They were odd creatures: human-shaped but small, no bigger than Peter himself. Their bodies and loose, streaming clothes changed colour with the sea, and that was why Peter hadn't noticed them before. Just now they were a hazy turquoise flecked with white, exactly matching the sea behind. Peter was used to seeing the Seafolk now and then, alone or in twos or threes, standing on the rocks by the shore, or on the lonely reefs out to sea where the villagers went to fish. But he had never seen so many together at once, and he had never been so close.

He wondered whether they could hear the voice too. As he watched, a larger wave than usual broke over the rocks with a terrible, long-drawn moan of sadness. The whole mass of Seafolk whispered and stirred, and then, to Peter's horror, they began to chant.

From all along the shore the sound came, and he saw that the whole Island was ringed with Seafolk, hundreds of them, whole armies, standing unseen, singing with the sea. Their song welled up with the murmur of the waves and flew round and round him on the freshening breeze.

The song of the Seafolk was a song of disaster. They sang of hurricane and whirlpool, of flood and fire and the downfall of islands, and the death of sea and land. And Peter knew that the words of the Seafolk's song were the same ones he had been straining to hear in the voice of the waves.

A sudden gust of wind nearly knocked him down. He glanced sharply out to sea. Without his noticing, a fresh stormcloud had climbed swiftly from the horizon, and was driving towards him, eating the sunset and swallowing the sky. The voices of the Seafolk rose to a roar.

'The seas will run dry, the wind will fall still,
and fire will burn under mountain and hill;
yet far we must travel, by thunder and snow,
where the summons is calling us: hark! We must go!'

Peter staggered back. He'd been right. Something dreadful was coming, something so terrible he could hardly imagine it. His home was in danger—his home, and perhaps the whole world of the sea . . . He had to get back home, right away, and warn them . . . But then the Seafolk suddenly turned round. They were gazing straight at him. Their bodies and clothes were grey-green, the colour of storms; and their faces were wild.

For a few moments Peter and the Seafolk simply stared at each other. The sky was darkening all the time; an eerie green twilight crept from the sea over the Island. In those few seconds Peter could hear the sound of the stormwinds whistling through the heather, and was aware of the sea answering to the gale, piling itself up into white-streaked hills.

Then the storm hit the Island. The wind boomed like thunder, throwing Peter off his feet. At the same moment the Seafolk let out a wild roar and came streaming up from the shore straight towards him. He picked himself up and ran. Behind him the waves crashed and screamed on the rocks, and the Seafolk swept on like a terrible, roaring flood. Peter leapt and scrambled up the Hill. What were they doing? The Seafolk never left the sea . . . If he could only get to the top, he thought, he'd be safe. They'd surely keep to the wild side of the Island—they wouldn't come into the village . . .

He had got about halfway, sprinting and leaping over the heather, with the swish and rush of the Seafolk right behind him; and there in front of him were the Shipstones, black against the storm . . . But beside the first of the stones he swerved to a halt. More Seafolk were coming straight towards him, over the top of the Hill; and there were other troops too, to right and left. In a few moments they'd meet, and he'd be caught.

Peter did the only thing he could. He slipped in between the Shipstones, and crouched behind one out of sight. He was only just in time. The swirling armies of Seafolk met like a joining of rivers, and swept round and over the place where he'd been. More and more kept coming, joining in the wailing, rolling dance, which now began to circle the stones. Their human shape was blurring in the storm; they were like rolling billows of water now, which flowed and moaned round him, sweeping wavelike fingers over the Shipstones as they passed. He gazed out in horror. He was trapped—and in the one place on the Island he'd been warned never to go.

Faster and faster the Seafolk swirled, wailing out their song against the crash of the waves and the wind's roar. Peter looked from the whirling, dancing figures to the clouds boiling past overhead, and reeled back, feeling dizzy. He tried to steady himself against the nearest pillar, but he jumped away in fear. The stone had moved.

All round him, the Shipstones were growing, probing upwards like slender trees. He stared in wonder, and cautiously reached out his hand. There was no mistake. He was touching not stone, but wood. Peter's heart was pounding. He knew he had to escape. But outside the Shipstones the dancing Seafolk still swirled, arms high, howling with the wind, their bodies merging in a green wall of water.

He nerved himself to charge through them, hoping somehow to break free. But before he could make himself move, there was a peeling, tearing shriek, like wood splitting. Planks sprang from the wooden posts at stem and stern, shooting round the ship's spars and riveting themselves in place. Peter clawed at the cage that was growing round him, but already the wooden walls were too high. Then came sounds like hammer blows from down by his feet. He jumped high as boards shot from the hull and snapped home against the planks opposite. He was standing on the deck of a ship.

Again the Seafolk roared, and the ship began to move. Peter ran to the side. He shouted with all his might, but the gale carried away his voice, and the ship lurched and threw him off his feet. On it bumped, at first slowly then faster, and Peter knew it was moving down to the sea.

He stared back from the bow, cold with horror, while a fresh shoot sprouted from the middle of the deck. Higher and higher it grew. A pair of branches shot from its sides, a bud formed between, swelled, then burst open, and a great grey sail unfurled like a young leaf. It filled at once with a wind of its own, and the ship sprang forward, straight into the teeth of the storm.

Close ahead, the breakers raged and pounded. Ragged sheets of spray glared white round the bows, and the ship paused on the sea's brink, trembling with the shock of the waves.

'Go back!' shouted Peter. 'We'll be killed!'

But the Seafolk roared their delight, and swarmed on board just as a breaker smashed over the rocks and floated them out from the shore. The ship dropped into a hollow among the waves. Black rocks reared all round, and white water fell seething back.

'Oars!' shouted Peter. 'Row clear of the rocks!'

But the Seafolk did not hear him. The next wave rose before them like a mountain, ready to sweep them back against the shore and smash the boat to pieces. Peter looked for an instant straight into the wave's green, gemlike heart, and then the ship rose on its crest, dived, and plunged out to sea.

The Seafolk cheered, and burst once more into their wailing, wordless song. At the sound of their voices the sail filled, and the ship flew on into the storm. The Island vanished behind. All round were great mountains of water, breaking in crests of foam which were torn away on the wind.

Peter slumped in the bows, his hands over his ears to drown the sound of the sea. 'Where are you going?' he wailed, and this time one of the Seafolk noticed him.

'A landsman!'

The others stopped singing and turned to stare.

'What does a landsman do here, out on the wild waves, in the sea's song?'

'No matter why he's here,' another said. 'A stranger's welcome to share the storm.'

A green monster of a wave rose over them. For a moment the bow slewed round, and the boat wallowed uneasily. Then the Seafolk returned to their song, the sail filled again and the ship leapt forward, cutting through the wave and drenching the deck with spray.

'Blow, wind, blow!' chanted the Seafolk. 'More sail and more sail! Faster and still faster!'

'But where are you *going*?' called Peter again, in agony.

One of the Seafolk turned to him.

'To sea! To sea! To the endless sea!'

'Where the storms breed and the whales play,' added a second, and they all began to chant:

> 'A thousand leagues from land,
> a thousand fathoms deep,
> where the hungry howling hurricane
> wakes dragons from their sleep!'

The crew cheered. Peter fell back against the thwart, staring blankly out over the sea. Foam and spray filled the air. All round was a changing terrain of watery crags and valleys: like the Mainland, he thought, with its great snow-topped mountains, and the terrible dark caves through their hearts where the miners dig for gold.

Then he saw something else: a black shape off in the water.

'Reefs!' he yelled. 'Turn her about!'

He knew that land of any sort was death in a storm. And there was another, and another; the things were all round them. They seemed to be dipping and rising and rolling on through the waves, keeping pace with the ship. The Seafolk began to cheer and point.

Then Peter knew what they were. The storm had stirred the sea to its depths, and the whales had come up to play. Suddenly he was cheering too, and all the danger of storm and sea were forgotten.

'To sea!' he found himself shouting, and his voice joined with those of the Seafolk. 'To sea! To sea! The endless sea!'

The ship flew on. The waves and the wind roared around them, and the air filled with spray and foam until there was no telling what was sky and what was sea. The ship climbed crest after crest, and behind each crest there always came another; and all the time Peter stood in the bow and gazed ahead, while the Seafolk sang and the storm howled, and the whales played alongside.

2

The Cave of Holla

When Peter woke next morning he was lying on a hard, damp floor. A dim, green light showed him he was in a room made of ancient, gleaming driftwood, which creaked and strained with a gentle motion. With a shock he remembered. He was in the Ship of Stones, and he was heading out to sea, with no idea where he was bound. For all he knew he might sail on and on, through storm after storm, until, long years later perhaps, the ship beached itself on another lonely island in some unknown sea far from home. He imagined himself, stranded, while the ship's planks rotted and disappeared, and its spars slowly turned back into stone . . .

He jumped up with a start. A creeping, scuttling sound had come from close by his side. He looked round, and now he saw the whole room was teeming with creatures. Crabs pattered among clogged clumps of weed, while sea-snails and whelks oozed across the walls and ceiling. From dark pools in the corners came the slither and swish of unseen things.

He set off hurriedly down a dim passageway. He had to find the crew—if there still was one. Other holds opened up on either side, and all were shadowed and slimy, crawling and creeping with the things of the sea like a great, moving rockpool. At last a shaft of brighter light fell in front of him, and he climbed a companionway up into the open air. And there, blue as a calm sea, he saw the Seafolk. They were moving restlessly over the deck, sniffing the wind or inspecting the sail. There was no land in sight.

'Our landsman!' one of them called out, seeing Peter, and the others turned to look.

'No,' laughed a second, a wild, playful-looking one with white, foam-like fingers. 'A true thing of the sea, to sleep in a storm!'

Peter felt himself grow bolder. 'Where are you taking me?' he demanded. 'I want to go home!'

At this, their laughter vanished. Then one, who was taller than the rest and looked like their captain, said, 'There's no going home any more. Not for anyone.'

'Why not? What do you mean?'

'Never again,' chanted the playful one. 'Only on, and forever on, into the wild and wonderful storm! To be at sea again, in the ship of stones, after all these ages!'

'Be quiet, Sosip,' said one of the others. 'Let Segrim tell him.' They all turned to face their leader.

'We're gathering,' said Segrim. 'That's what the ship's for.'

Peter stared at him. 'And that's why you called the storm?'

'Ah,' said Sosip. 'We don't call storms. If we only could! But we can use them, for our launching and our gathering.'

The other Seafolk hushed Sosip to be quiet, and Segrim went on.

'At the start of time, the things of the sea set out in seven ships from the place where they were given life. One ship sailed to each of the seven seas of the world, carrying the creatures that were to live there. After that the ships' task was done, and each one beached on a lonely island and turned to stone. From that day the ships of the sea have waited, ready in case of need. And now at last the summons has gone out. All of us have felt it. The Ships of

Stones are gathering the things of the sea, back to their old home, from each of the seven seas—back to the Cave of Holla.'

'But *why*?' Peter stared round at the silent, blue-white figures of the Seafolk, who looked solemnly back at him. Then he said, 'Is it to do with the voice in the sea?'

At this a murmur spread through the Seafolk. They swayed over the deck like waves, and Peter remembered their dance around the Shipstones, and was afraid.

'He knows,' whispered one. 'He's heard.'

'Please,' begged Peter, 'I know you can hear it too. The song you sang on the rocks—it was the sea's voice put into words, wasn't it? Please! What does it mean?'

The Seafolk murmured, and flitted one behind the other, grey as the sea in a storm; but Segrim looked at Peter steadily. 'We gave words to the waves' wail, and speech to the sea's singing. What we heard, we sang, and the song made us afraid; yet we know nothing of what the song might mean, any more than you. But Holla will know. Holla will tell us, when we go to her.'

The Seafolk behind him were dancing more and more like a wall of water, and now began to chant, 'Holla, Holla . . .'

'Who *is* Holla?' begged Peter.

'Holla?' repeated Segrim in surprise. 'Holla is Queen of the Sea.'

The Seafolk gradually subsided back into man-shapes and moved once more about their duties. Peter asked no more questions. He had begun to see some hope again. Holla would tell them what the song of the sea meant. And if she was Queen of the Sea, she would certainly be able to stop its suffering, and prevent the terrible prophecy he had heard from coming true.

He leant his head against the rail, and gazed thoughtfully out over the sea. Off in the distance he could still see the whales, keeping pace with the ship, and now there were other creatures too. Seals sported in the water, jumping across the bows, dolphins leapt alongside, and schools of fish flashed below the surface. There were swordfish and narwhals, and other things, just glimpsed: the great, smiling, scaly sea-satyr, raising his bearded head; the sea-unicorn, and the monkfish, cloaked and cowled; strange dwellers in far-flung seas.

There were Seafolk too. They appeared as if from the foam of the waves, and swarmed up the sides of the ship to join the crew. Other sea-beasts were with them. Crabs and sand-worms, sea-slugs and limpets crept everywhere over the deck, scuttling and slithering down into the friendly cool of the holds.

Then, late in the day, a cry went up from the Seafolk. Looking ahead over the bows, Peter saw a cluster of strange, twisted islands. Some made arches that a ship could have passed through, and some leant like lopsided towers, ready to collapse; and in the middle of them all was a single island peak, rising above the rest like a citadel over the roofs of a town.

Gradually the ship drew nearer, until they passed among the dark, echoing cliffs of the outer islands. The sea here was thronged with creatures. They clambered and crept, hopped and waddled over the rocks, and shot through the sea-caves in glittering shoals; and all were moving with a single purpose, towards the great castle-like island in the centre.

And now the island rose before them, buttress on buttress, with pinnacles and pillars marching up its sides, and stairs cut in the cliffs twining up and around past innumerable hollows and caves. At the island's foot were seven docks, and at each of these put in a great driftwood ship. Peter stepped out on to the rock along with his ship's crew, dazed by the din and the confusion of creatures.

Then he felt himself swept forward. Like a rising tide, the Seafolk were swarming together into the great cave in the island's heart.

The cave was huge. A sea-green light, like that in the ship, shone down in shafts from openings in the rocks high above, and all around was the sound of the wind, groaning down the island's tunnels as if through organ pipes. The Seafolk's murmuring fell silent, and their faces all turned the same way. Then Peter saw.

Across the other side of the cave, seated on a great blue-white throne, was a tall, grand, sad-looking lady. She looked old, but beautiful, and her face and hands were as white and worn as driftwood. She gazed out over the cave, as if listening for something, and a fresh murmur ran through the Seafolk.

'Holla . . . Holla . . . Holla . . . '

The murmuring grew to a roar, loud as the sea, then slowly died again. Then seven of the Seafolk stood forward and approached the throne. One of them was Segrim, and Peter guessed that the rest were the captains of the other six ships.

The captains bowed, and one of them spoke.

'We have come, my Lady. We felt your call: we have heard the sadness of the sea's singing, and have all seen our Ships of Stone launched into the storm. The things of the sea have gathered. And now, my Lady, we would willingly know what you command, and why you have summoned us.'

Holla gazed down at them sadly. 'You have come,' she said at last, 'and the things of the sea have gathered. You have been summoned, yes; but it was not I who summoned you.'

A murmur ran through the cave, and the Seafolk swayed in agitation, like a still pool when a squall of wind falls on it. The captains looked at each other, troubled.

'But then, my Lady,' asked Segrim, 'who did?'

Holla held up her hand for quiet. 'There is a voice,' she said, 'a voice which calls to me, summoning me from my home. I hear it even now, forever whispering and tugging, soft, cunning, never-wearying. "Come," it whispers, "Come." It is something apart from the voice of the sea, something away and beyond, and the sea only partly understands it. It is this summons that has brought you here in your seven ships, and still it calls us on, drawing us away, further, further. I turn my mind against it, and for a time I can hold back. But its strength is greater than my own. In the end I must follow. And you, my subjects, must follow too.'

'Where? Where?' begged the captains.

Holla slowly shook her head. 'I do not know. I have asked the sea: I have listened to the wisdom of the waves. And the voice of the sea sings of doom, of doom and the death of the waters. But more than this it cannot tell me. This call is outside the sea's wisdom, over and away beyond. The waves' voice cannot say who is calling us, or where, or why.'

The whispers of the Seafolk ran round and round on the echoes. The captains had sunk down from the throne like a wave, hissing and tumbling back in fear; but now they broke forward again in anger.

'And will the sea die?'

'Is there no help for us?'

'No means of learning, of finding who, or why . . . '

'Tell us!'

Once more the Queen of the Sea raised her hand, and she sighed with a sound like the sea rippling over the shore.

'There is a way . . . A new wisdom is needed: a wisdom beyond that of the sea. Far away on the Mainland, high up in the mountains among the rocks and the snow, there lives a hermit. He is said to be wiser than all the creatures of the world, and to know all there is to be known of earth and air, fire and sea. His wisdom may reach far enough.'

A rising growl of horror broke from the Seafolk. They began to wail and sway, their bodies a troubled, angry green, and in their murmuring Peter heard one phrase repeated over and over. 'The land . . . the land . . . '

The captains surged back from the throne in impatience.

'But, my Lady, the land! The mountains!'

'The terrible, dry places!'

'The journey would be death!'

Holla gave a sad nod. 'We may be summoned to death all the same. But you are right. No creature of the sea can go on this quest. Only a land creature might save us—a thing of the land who loves the sea.'

The seven captains turned angrily away, flowing back among the crowd.

'Impossible!'

'Land loves land!'

'None but the Seafolk sigh for the sea!'

Peter stared over the heads of the troubled Seafolk. A horrible sense of dread was rising up in him. Holla had no answer. No one could do anything about it—except him. It would be terrible, journeying up into the Mainland, up among the mountains and the snow. He'd heard the stories the Islanders told, how the land there went on forever, valley on valley, mountain on mountain, crests of stone and seas of rock; endless, unmoving earth in place of the beautiful, changing sea; and all of it unknown, and teeming with strange creatures . . .

Yes, it would be terrible. But for the Seafolk the journey would be death. And then he thought of the Island, of his father and mother, of Lotta and Kari, and all the other villagers . . . it was his chance to save his home—to save the sea. Kari wouldn't have hesitated, he thought, if she'd been the one. But she wasn't. There was no one but him. Almost without realizing he was doing it, he rose to his feet and began to walk forward towards the throne.

The Seafolk fell back from him like the tide, whispering, and Peter walked on, down an avenue of bare rock between swaying green forms. At last he stood at the foot of the throne. Holla bent down to him gently.

'Welcome, land creature! Or is it land *and* sea? Neither and both?'

'I . . . I don't know, your Majesty,' Peter answered. 'But I do love the sea.'

A whisper went through the cave, and Holla said, 'If you love it, will you save it?'

'If I can—If you tell me where I have to go.'

'You must go to the place where the land closes in and the sea stops, where the mountains rise up, high as the sea is deep. To the land: land without end.'

A low sigh of horror rose from the Seafolk. Holla went on. 'It is a dry road to travel, up and up from the sea, to the heights where the hermit dwells. Will you? Will you go? And learn of a Reprieve from the Summons?'

The Seafolk seemed to be holding their breaths. For a long moment there was no sound at all but the dismal howling of the wind in the caves.

'Yes,' he said. 'I'll go.'

Holla sighed. The Seafolk roared their approval with a sound like a hurricane. One of the Ships of Stones glided forward to a dark, underground pier, and the watery arms of the Seafolk swept Peter aboard.

3
Land Without End

The Ship of Stones glided out among the islands into the evening calm. For a time, Peter kept watch, while the twisted spires of Holla's island dwindled behind, making home seem further away than ever. And then, when the stars were out and there was no land in sight, he fell asleep.

When he woke, it was broad daylight, and the Seafolk were prowling over the deck, grey and troubled.

'What is it?' Peter asked, struggling to his feet, but the Seafolk only turned and stared ahead over the bow. And then he saw. It was land, vast and mountainous, towering up like stormclouds. Dark forest swarmed up the slopes, silver waterfalls streaked down from bare summits; and behind those mountains he could see the glint of others, higher, grander, their peaks hidden in snow and ice. Peter shuddered. It was horrifying. The land was bigger than anything he could have imagined. And somehow he would have to journey into it.

Still the ship carried on, as if Segrim meant them to crash straight into the rock. But at the last moment a way opened up between the cliffs. The ship passed into shadow, and the land closed round them. The great open sea which Peter had always known was shut in, imprisoned: a narrow channel, snaking deeper and deeper into the mountains. Even the water looked wrong. It lay still and green, mirroring the land.

'How much longer?' he whispered.

But Segrim only shook his head. 'We go on, and we go on, until the sea stops. We do not know.'

'It's so dark!' Peter protested. 'And the sea: it's not like sea at all! It should move, and flow. It shouldn't just be still. It's got no voice!'

'It dares not speak,' answered Segrim, 'where the land leans over, listening.'

'When you take to the Mainland,' another added, 'your way will be worse.'

Peter heaved a sigh, and went on gazing ahead, at the water that looked like land, and the dark, menacing cliffs. Round one bend after another the ship sailed, and always the sea wound on; and then suddenly the cliffs drew back, the channel made one last turn, and the sea ran up to a shingly beach and stopped. Beyond was only land: thick forest, and a valley that climbed steeply into the mountains.

The ship glided forward until its prow was touching the beach, and then it too came to a stop. All was silence. Peter glanced at his guides, and at the way ahead. It was a dreadful moment, leaving the ship, the sea, and his companions: everything that still linked him to home. But he had better get it over with. He jumped down on to the shore. He was on the Mainland now—not just an island, but land that went on and on, unending. He turned to look back. The Seafolk gazed sadly down on him; then the ship slid off over the dark water, and slowly turned her nose to the sea.

Peter watched the ship go with a sinking feeling. He was alone now: really alone, and out of his element, a sea-thing stranded on the land. It was mad. What could he do? If only the whole thing had never happened, and he could have stayed safe at home on the Island . . . But thinking like that was no use. He had to go on, and save his home if he could.

He turned and faced the valley. Land was ahead of him: land without end. Rocks and trees came spilling down the mountainsides into the valley bottom, where a rushing stream flowed out over the beach. Nearby, a faint track led up into the forest. There was nothing for it. He plunged into the trees along the path.

At first he ran and ran, just for the strange new pleasure of running, and knowing there was no seashore just over the hill to stop him. But after a time he had to slow down. It was hot. Flies buzzed in the sun, and above him the clouds surged strangely in sudden gusts of wind. Did clouds always churn like that over the land? Anything might be normal here, and yet seem strange. Every sight and smell was new, and each one had some meaning; but that meaning was like the voice of the sea, and eluded him.

He walked on more slowly, craning up to look at the cliffs, which reared over him like the face of the sea set on end. Boulders dotted the slopes, great pieces of rock as big as islands, tiny in the vastness of the mountains. Stone was all round him, leaning over him, crouching under him, fathoms deep below his feet; wormed through, perhaps, with tunnels and mines.

'I'm a thing of the sea,' he whispered, shuddering. 'I'm like the Seafolk. This isn't my place.'

He ran on. His heart was beating fast. At every scuffle in the undergrowth he started, and then he came round a bend in the path and stopped dead.

In front of him, sitting in a great dead tree like a skeleton, was a flock of gaunt, staring birds. Yellow eyes bored into him. 'The secrets of the mountains are ours,' the eyes seemed to say. 'We know them: you don't.'

Peter blinked to break their stare, and ran on. 'Birds,' he panted. 'Just birds. They were owls . . . or something. Mustn't panic.'

He toiled on up through the trees, but soon he had a fresh shock. Where the way led beside the foot of a cliff there was a kind of cave, with a confused mass of footprints leading out of it and up the path ahead. Peter stood and stared in horror. The prints had been made by narrow, pointed feet, and each one was burnt deep into the ground.

In a moment he was running again, up and on; and all along the path ran the singed, steaming footmarks too, keeping pace with him.

'*Mustn't* panic,' he gasped as he ran. 'Probably . . . quite normal . . . for the land. *Mustn't* be afraid . . . *must* find the hermit.'

The weather had changed. Drizzling banks of mist hung before the cliffs, and the forest was filled with the gentle patter of rain. It sounded just like running footsteps. Peter ran and ran, his eyes on the terrible singed marks under his feet. And now came a fresh terror. A new kind of footprint had joined the others, and these had been made by cloven hoofs.

Trembling all over, Peter burst from the trees into a grassy clearing, and before he knew it the monsters were all round him. Their yellow eyes rolled, their jaws champed and munched, and long, narrow faces pressed up to him, nudging him with curling horns. Peter stood rock-still in a sea of shaggy bodies, not daring to move, expecting every moment to feel the beasts begin to tear him apart.

Then, over the backs of the monsters, he saw a girl. She was coming towards him, just as if the terrible creatures were invisible to her.

'Get away!' Peter yelled. 'Save yourself!'

But the girl only kept coming, quite unconcerned. She strode in among the beasts and gave a whistle, and the monsters trotted apart in different directions. Peter stared at her in amazement.

'How did you do that?'

'It's easy,' replied the girl, who was about Peter's age, and dark and strong-looking. 'What's wrong? Haven't you seen a goat before?'

Peter felt his knees go weak with relief.

'Goats! Were they *goats*?'

The girl stared, and then she laughed. 'Don't worry. They won't eat *you*. Just your clothes.' Peter turned round in time to snatch his sleeve from one of the creature's jaws.

'Well, how was I to know? They don't have goats where I come from.' He eyed the beast's champing mouth uneasily. 'You're *sure* they're not dangerous?'

'Of course not. They're just always eating. Look, if you hold their horns you can feel it.' She rested her hand on the horn of an uncomplaining goat, and Peter reached gingerly out to do the same.

'Except not that one,' the girl warned him. 'That's Old Billy. He'd butt you. What's your name?'

'I'm Peter.'

'And I'm Elsa.' She looked him up and down. 'Where *do* you come from?'

'From the sea: from an island.'

'And what brings you to the mountains?'

He hesitated, unsure how much to tell her. But he needed someone to trust. 'I'm on a quest. I'm looking for a wise man who lives in these mountains. I need his help.'

Elsa looked thoughtful. 'A wise man. That would be Grandfather. But you mustn't call him that,' she warned. '*He* doesn't think he's wise at all.'

She turned to the goats, and called them together with another whistle. 'Well, I can see you're a bit out of your element, Peter from the Sea. I'd better give you a hand.'

'Just tell me the way,' said Peter. 'I'll manage.'

'Will you? With all the forest creeping with creatures, and everywhere all fidgety and wakeful? It's not as if things are normal just now, you know.'

Peter's mind ran back over the great staring bird-creatures, the fiery footprints . . .

'So the land *isn't* always like this?'

Elsa shook her head. 'Things are on the move. The animals are restless—flocking together when they don't normally. Even the goats are jumpy. And there are queer things about. Night things are out in the day—underground things, too. They're gathering.'

Peter's heart jumped. 'Did you say *gathering*?'

'Odd things—things that ought to stay hidden. Why?'

'It's just . . . the sea things are gathering too. There's a voice—it calls to them, summoning them, whispering to them to come. And they've got to obey.'

Elsa frowned. 'And what is this voice? Where are they being summoned *to*?'

Peter shook his head. 'No one knows. But it's bad. And if the same thing's happening here . . . '

They both stood a moment in silence, pondering. Then Elsa said, 'Well, you come with me. I'll take you to Grandfather. *He'll* know what it all means.'

A roll of thunder boomed from the mountains, and drizzle began to patter among the trees.

'We'd better hurry. There's rain coming, and it's a bit of a climb.'

They set off, with the goats trotting patiently after them. The path wound up the steep valley side, and the stream became a torrent, rushing along deep below.

'I'm in charge of the practical side,' Elsa was saying. 'I bring the goats down to pasture and all that, and Grandfather sees to the thinking. That's why he has to live so high up in the mountains. Down here the air's too heavy. He says his thoughts get all squashed and cramped.'

Peter suddenly stopped.

'What is it?' asked Elsa.

'I thought I heard something.'

'It's just the rain.'

'Possibly . . .'

Then they both heard. A sound of scorching and sizzling was coming from behind them. They turned. Fiery shapes were racing up the path towards them, still a good way off, but coming rapidly closer. Steam billowed from the wet ground where their burning feet touched it. The goats scattered in fright, and Peter was still staring in horror when Elsa dragged him off the path and into the forest.

4
Fire and Hail

'Quick!' Elsa commanded. 'Up this tree!'

'But what about the goats?'

'They'll find their way home all right. It's us I'm worried about.'

Peter gazed down the path, and up at the tree. The trunk looked horribly smooth and difficult. 'You want me to *climb* this?'

'Yes. Come on, quick!'

'You sound like my little sister, Kari. She's always trying to get me to do really impossible things, too.'

'Thanks a lot! I'm not asking you to climb this tree for *fun*, you know! Hurry *up*!'

'All right. How?'

'*How?*'

'Yes, how. I've never climbed a tree before.'

'Never climbed a *tree*! What sort of misspent childhood have you been *having*?'

'If you tried climbing any of the trees on our island, you'd pull them up by the roots. I don't suppose *you* know how to swim.'

Elsa snorted. 'In what? The stream's only ankle-deep.'

'Well, what *are* we going to do? They're coming!'

'All right, never mind not knowing how. Up!' Elsa seized him by the scruff of the neck and gave him a hoist and a shove up into the tree. She swarmed up after him, and just as they settled themselves among the branches, three short, fiery creatures scorched their way up the path below them and came to a halt. Wisps of flame flickered from their bodies, which hissed and steamed in the rain. They looked horribly angry.

'Scorch and fry this freezing damp!' snarled one. 'We'll be extinguished! Snuffed out, before we've even time to gather!'

'Best shelter, say I,' another answered. 'I've taken all I can of it.'

'So say I!' put in the third.

Peter carefully pushed aside some leaves, and peered down at the blazing shapes. 'Do you know what they are?' he whispered.

'They're fire goblins,' hissed Elsa back. 'Firefolk. Now quiet!'

Steaming and grumbling, the creatures crept under the tree where Peter and Elsa were hiding, and huddled together in a glowing mass.

'Watch out!' snapped one. 'Burn the tree down, and where's our shelter?'

'I wish we'd never left!' groaned the second.

'We had to, didn't we?' returned the third.

'That's right. Brand called us.'

'Well, why did he? Dark and deep we were, snugged down safe in the fire under the mountain!'

'Perhaps he saw something, in the wisdom of the fire.'

'Brand knows. Brand is Lord of Fire. Brand will guide us.'

Thunder rolled and echoed round the mountains. The fire creatures shuddered. Just then a cold gust of wind swept past the tree and a cloud brushed overhead, shedding a tremendous shower of hail right on top of them. Giant bullet-shaped hailstones bounced over the ground, and the fire goblins leapt up with yells of rage, shaking their glowing fists at the sky.

'Just wait! Just you wait!'

'Brand's coming!'

'He'll scorch the rain, and fry the fog!'
'Burn the clouds and bake the earth!'
'Turn this whole soggy mess to a blazing desert!'
'*Then* we'll have a world that's fit to live in!'
'So say I!'
'And I!'

Peter risked another peek, but a swirl of steam blew up past him, and a tickle got into his nose. He rubbed it and wrinkled it, but it was no use. He drew in a few huge breaths, and then he sneezed. Elsa looked at him, horrified and reproachful, and down below the fire goblins jumped.

'What was that?'
'It was the tree.'
'It sneezed.'
'Idiot! Trees don't sneeze!'
'Big expert! How do you know?'
'Yes, ever see a tree before today? No! I thought not!'
'I tell you it was a land-thing. A nasty, damp, creeping land-thing. I hate 'em. Next one I find, I'll fry it for dinner, and no questions asked!'
'Silly! You can't *eat* the things. They're all wet and horrible.'
'Well, I'll fry it anyway, for spite.'
'Well, there'll be no more wet once Brand comes, not anywhere, not ever. And a good thing!'

The first goblin yawned. 'So say I!'
'And I,' murmured the second.
'This cold . . . '
'Mustn't go to sleep . . . '
'How long till we join the main band?'
'Not long, not long.'
'And they'll find a way up the big cliff: that's what they said.'
'But there's time yet . . . '

The hissing yawns grew louder and longer. Peter looked down at the heaving mass of goblin, their folded arms, caps, and buttons blurring together like the glowing coals in a fire. He leant over to Elsa and whispered, 'They're asleep.'

Elsa put her finger to her lips, and lowered herself silently to the ground. Peter struggled down, branch by branch, and dropped clumsily by her side. He spun round to look at the goblins, but they were still snoozing and smouldering quietly. Elsa beckoned. They picked their way carefully along the path, then broke into a sprint.

'Fire goblins!' Peter repeated when they slowed down. 'Where do they come from? What are they doing here?'

Elsa shook her head. 'Don't know. But judging by the footprints, I'd say they're oozing up everywhere, through all the cracks in the earth. We'd better hurry. If we meet any of them on the cliff path, we'll be in trouble.'

She led them on at a faster pace, and then they came round a corner and stopped dead. Sitting in front of them was an angrily staring creature, goblin-sized, and whitish-grey all over.

'Fire goblin!' Peter shouted, trying to pull Elsa back.

Elsa stood her ground. 'Can't be. It's not burning.'

'Well, maybe it's gone out. Quick, let's go round, before it does something.'

All this time the goblin stared at them harder and harder, its eyes bulging with rage.

'Fire goblin?' it burst out at last. '*Fire* goblin? I've got nothing to do with *fire*! If it was up to me, all the fire in the world would be put out. *And* all the mountains knocked flat, too.'

'Well, what are you then?' Peter asked, still hanging back.

The creature gave a sniff of contempt. 'A hail goblin, of course. Moke's the name.' It sat up and bowed, sweeping off its sharply pointed hat to reveal a sharply pointed head underneath. 'And what, might I ask, are you?'

'We're people,' said Peter. 'Children.'

Moke sized them up with another sniff. 'Well, you're very ugly ones.'

Elsa turned to Peter. 'Look, we haven't got time to stand here talking to goblins. The rain's stopping. That means the Firefolk will wake up. Are you coming, or not?'

Instantly, Moke's manner changed. 'Firefolk?' repeated the hail goblin fearfully. 'Where? Are they near?'

'Down the path,' answered Elsa. 'Come on, Peter.'

'It's just I helped dump a load of hail on some,' Moke explained, 'and they might not be very pleased about it. We'd better go.'

'That's what I *said*,' retorted Elsa, and strode off. Moke followed, casting nervous glances back. Peter shook himself and ran after them. There was something he had to understand.

'Wait! Elsa! Don't you see?'

'See what?'

'How strange it is. Do you normally get hail goblins here? Down on the ground?'

'No,' Elsa admitted. 'No, never.'

Peter turned to Moke.

'You said you'd just been dropping hailstones. What were you doing sitting on that rock?'

Moke scowled. 'I was sulking.'

'Why?'

'Why! *There's* a question. Well: I'd been stuck in the back room as usual, casting hailstones—'

'Throwing them, you mean?'

'No, not *throwing* them: casting them. Making them in a mould. Melting offcuts of snow and ice over a little fire made of coldness—then you pour them into pointed moulds—'

'Shaped like your head, in other words,' interrupted Elsa from up in front. 'If you're coming, just don't lag behind, that's all.'

Moke glared, and went on. 'Well, then we started divebombing those nasty firecreatures—'

'*Why?*' Peter interrupted.

'Why? I don't know why. Orders. I'm not some great sky-general or storm-courtier. Hagal doesn't tell *me* his plans.'

'Hagal?'

Moke stared. 'The Lord of Storms.'

So there was another one.

'Well? And then?'

'So there we were. Well, everyone else was working the gadgets and pulling the cranks, whooping and pointing, and me with my ladle and pot in the back room, pouring 'em in, chucking 'em out—you've got to do a thousand years of that before they let you drive, and I'd only done a hundred. And Clatter got to work the hail chute and Slodkin was driving—and nine hundred years still to do, and the back room doesn't even have a *window*—and so then . . . I . . . finally . . . had ENOUGH!'

Moke paused dramatically, and Peter had to say, 'Well? *Then* what?'

'I put down the ladle,' said Moke with relish, 'and came through to the cockpit. There they all were, laughing away at the controls. I just said, quiet-like, "I want my turn." So then they tell me to get back to my ladle, and Bludgeon tells me I'm only a goblin third class, and he's second class with stars. Well, at this point they weren't watching the knobs and gadgetry, so I charge in, take hold, and next thing we're zooming past the target, bombs away with a full load (that was Slodkin: he fell on the lever)—'

'That was *us*,' put in Elsa. 'We were in the tree.'

'Very likely,' retorted Moke icily. 'Anyway, we weave about a bit, knock into this and that, then the others pick themselves up and all of a sudden Slodkin's clinging round my neck and Clatter's nobbling me over the head with the ladle. Well of *course* I couldn't steer with all *that* going on, and someone had parked a mountain right where we were heading. So we nosedive, smashcrash, all fall out, and I roll down and end up on a rock. *That's* why I was sulking.'

'You really are a trouble-maker, aren't you?' said Elsa. Moke was swelling up ready for some angry reply when Elsa suddenly stopped. Peter looked up, shaken from his worried brooding, and let out a whistle of dismay.

A great ring of cliffs faced them, rising sheer into the clouds. Drifts of mist floated down across the rockfaces, some of them almost reaching the ground.

Peter scanned the dizzying reaches of stone in panic. 'You said there was a path!'

'The path's up there.' Elsa pointed to a narrow line scratched across the cliff. To Peter it looked terrifying. But there was worse. When he squinted hard, he could make out points of fire moving along it, like long lines of sparks.

'Firefolk,' he murmured.

Elsa nodded. 'So that's no good.'

'Well, so what do we do now? Is there some other way up?'

Elsa shook her head and frowned. 'I'm thinking.'

'You'd better come up with something quite soon,' hummed Moke, 'because the rain's really *really* stopped now, and the Firefolk are coming.'

Elsa glared at him. 'Why can't *you* think of something, instead of just complaining and spoiling things?'

'It's your job to think of something, because you're in charge,' Moke explained.

'Don't you just have a wonderful attitude to life? You go dropping hail on people for no reason, making them angry, and it's *my* job to sort it out!'

'Dropping hail's what I'm *for*,' retorted Moke. 'Besides, it's fun.'

'Fun! If you think—'

'Look,' ordered Peter. 'There's no time for arguing. Let's just keep moving. Maybe if we get a bit nearer the cliffs something will turn up.'

They hurried on, through wisps of drizzling fog. When Peter glanced back he could see a column of steam rising from beyond the brow of the slope, with the occasional flash of fire glaring underneath. They had almost reached the foot of the cliff when Moke suddenly let out a cry and galloped forward, vanishing into a low bank of mist that lay draped over the path.

'Where's he gone now?' grumbled Elsa.

The hail goblin's head reappeared at a kind of window in the fog.

'It's my cloud! Come on!'

Peter and Elsa stopped and stared at the hazy wall of whiteness, which looked just like any other bank of mist. It certainly didn't look safe to travel in.

'Are you sure it's yours?' asked Peter.

Moke bounced out and ran his frosty fingers lovingly over the cloud's surface. 'Of course I'm sure! That's the dent we gave it last year when we tried to sink the king's fishing fleet. Got tangled in the rigging. But that wasn't *my* fault. It was Slodkin started it.' He patted the cloud's side with a gentle thud. 'Seems all right. There's your answer: we *fly* over the cliffs, and yah boo to the Firefolk.'

'Us?' said Peter. 'In that? I mean, it's just a cloud. What's it made of?'

'Light model like this? Air, mostly, with sleet reinforcing rods. Zappy little number. Just wait till I get her started.'

Moke disappeared again behind a fold in the mist. Peter and Elsa looked at each other.

'Well,' said Peter, 'it's this or the Firefolk . . . '

They followed Moke cautiously. Inside the cloud it was cold, and brilliantly white. Moke was busily fiddling with various cranks and rods and levers, which ran back through the foggy sides of the cloud like deformed icicles. A shadowy doorway led through into the back room, where Peter saw Moke's abandoned ladle and cauldron, with a bin full of finished hailstones. Beside them was a lever, and a sign saying:

CAUTION: HAIL CHUTE. DO NOT LEAN OUT.

There was a window above, and through it Peter saw the Firefolk, a great band of them, roaring towards them like wildfire. He ran back to the cockpit.

'Hurry!' he shouted. 'They're coming!'

Moke was winding pulleys and yanking knobs, ever more desperately.

'You don't know how to drive it, do you?' stated Elsa.

From outside they heard the hissing of fire and steam, and the crackle of the Firefolk's voices. They had nearly reached them.

'There, in that cloud!'

'Sky creatures!'

'They thought they'd quench us!'

'They'll fry and frazzle, for that!'

'Rot and quench them!' cursed Moke. 'Something's stuck—rods and gadgets all jammed—'

'Do something!' commanded Elsa.

'And quick!' added Peter.

'*You* do something,' Moke snapped back.

Peter looked round in desperation at the frosty knobs and levers, and then one of them caught his eye. It was big and knobbly, and scratched on its icy surface was the word 'GO'. He darted forward and pressed it. Fire flashed through the room, and steam scorched from the doorway where the Firefolk hit. But at the same moment the cloud gave a shudder and a bound, and whirled dizzily away into the air.

5
Lord of Storms

Peter fell backwards, and clutched desperately at a lever for support. The next thing he knew he was dangling from the hail chute half out of the cloud, with a full load of hailstones clattering out of their bin round his ears, and down over the furious Firefolk.

Hissing steam blinded him, mixed with shrieks of rage, and then the cloud tipped over, and Peter was thrown back inside. Bruised and dizzy, he crawled through into the cockpit, where Moke was crouched over the controls like a maniac, yanking every knob in sight.

'I did it! I did it!' he cackled, twirling rods and wiggling props. 'Look at me!'

The cloud danced wildly from side to side, and the cliffs leapt closer.

'Watch out!' yelled Elsa.

Moke glared at her, and twisted an icy-looking crankshaft. The cloud swerved away from the cliff, and shot out over the deep, misty void of the valley, back the way they had come.

'Turn around!' Elsa shouted.

'Not easy with all these cliffs,' Moke complained. 'We'll have to go up and over. You asked for it.'

He wound wheels and cranked cranks, and suddenly the cloud veered sharply upwards, throwing Peter off his feet again. Pinnacles of rock flashed by, and then they were looping the loop, all three yelling with terror. Back they flew past the cliffs, this time upside-down. Hailstones spilled out and rattled round their ears, and the cloud's struts and rods groaned with the strain.

'Turn . . . us . . . over!' panted Elsa, and grabbed the controls.

'No! I can do it!' shouted Moke, jabbing at a series of foot-pedals. Slowly the cloud righted itself and circled the cliffs, about halfway up. Round and round they went, higher each time, and now when Peter looked down he saw scorching trails of fire goblins approaching from several directions. Some of them were setting off up the narrow path scratched in the rockface, but others were gathering in a body at the foot of the cliff, near what looked like a group of caves. He wondered what they were planning to do.

Moke's exultant voice shrilled from the cockpit.

'Look at me! I'm flying! Flying!'

'Just to the top of the cliff, you're flying,' Elsa reminded him.

'A hundred years I waited! And it could have been a thousand!' Moke sighed with delight and pulled a handle. The cloud tipped back and soared steeply up over the edge of the cliffs. A cold wind pierced them, and now Peter could see ahead across a grey landscape of scrubby birches and wandering streams. Peaks stood all round. Snow lurked in the hollows of the hills, and in the distance lay a dazzling sea of ice. He wondered where in all this empty waste was the house of the hermit.

'Down there!' ordered Elsa. Right below them a stream wound down over the mountainside, with what looked like a large rock set in the middle of it. 'That's Grandfather's house. Put us down!'

But Moke wasn't listening. His face had taken on a blissful, dreamy look.

'Flying . . . a hundred years . . .'

The cloud was still circling, climbing and climbing.

Soon they were as far above the grey plateau as they had been above the valley.

'Moke!' called Peter. 'You can take us in to land now!'

Elsa seized Moke's arm and shouted in his ear. 'Land! Now!'

'Not yet!' Moke pleaded. 'Just a bit higher. Then I'll take you down. I promise. Just look!'

Elsa let go of his arm reluctantly. The ground had vanished; streaks of mist darted past outside. Then they were hit by a blinding sun, and towering masses of cloud rose like mountains around them.

'The Hall of Storms,' whispered Moke, pointing to a menacing mound of darkness which loomed behind the rest. 'Where the winds are brewed and the thunder's forged.' He gazed for a moment entranced, and then his pale face twisted into a scowl. 'But I've been this high before. I want to go higher!'

'Moke!' wailed Peter and Elsa together, but the goblin let out a whistle of glee, yanked at a lever or two, and sent the cloud soaring up into the wind so steeply that its rods rattled.

'You'll kill us!' shouted Peter.

'Higher! Higher! As high as the sun! As high as the stars!'

The towering city of clouds lay below, and still they climbed, spiralling up above the Hall of Storms. All around them the sky was a sparkling blue, empty but for a white, burning sun.

'This is glorious! Marvellous! Exquisite! Superb!'

'Listen to me, Moke!' shouted Peter. 'What happens if we go too high?'

'Beautiful—sublime—what?' Moke frowned. 'Yes . . . We are a bit near the sun, it's true. These light jobs aren't really made to stand the heat. In fact,' he went on, his frown growing deeper, 'you'd better check the rods aren't melting.'

Peter and Elsa exchanged one look of horror, and then both started yelling at once.

'Take us down! Now! Take us down!'

Moke scowled, and cast a sulky look up at the sun. 'All right, all right. Down, did you say?'

'Yes! Down!'

They were right over the black stormcloud, and Moke was gazing at it dreamily. 'Down . . . when the hailclouds gather, and the storm-trolls beat the drums for war . . . we mass in our ranks, and then we dive . . . like this!'

He threw the controls forward, and the cloud shot down through the air like a plummet. Wind screamed in their ears. The dark, roiling mass of the Hall of Storms seemed to rush up to meet them.

'No-o!' yelled Peter, and 'What happens if we hit it?' Elsa demanded.

'Don't care! A big smash! That'll show them if I'm fit to drive a cloud!'

'It certainly will,' muttered Peter.

Then Elsa tried to wrestle Moke away from the controls, and Peter took up the ladle and began hitting the goblin over the head with it, while all the time the wind screamed louder and the rods and cranks rattled and jarred. Moke kept his frosty fingers clenched on the steering-knob. Black streamers of cloud boiled up round them, and thunder boomed from beneath. Down and down they plunged, closer to the dark cloud and closer still. Sentinels peered at them from cloud-towers, and Peter had a glimpse of surprised, bearded faces pushing telescopes from misty windows. And then they hit.

There was a rending, tearing creak. Tatters of blackness wrapped themselves around the front of the hailcloud, but still they were going down, plunging through floor after floor, past thunder-stores and sleet-bins, hail-factories and snowmills, where storm-brewers looked up from their great icy vats, and hail goblins scattered in fright.

Every time they crashed through another storey there was a tremendous crunch and jar; but the cloud was going slower now, and at last it came to rest, sunk part-way through the floor of a vast, shadowy storeroom.

Peter and Elsa picked themselves up, dazed, while Moke still sat at the controls, staring blankly.

'You stupid, *stupid* goblin!' Elsa began, but Peter hushed at her to be quiet. He was peering down through the window, which was pressed into the floor where the cloud had tipped on its side. Only a thin layer of mist separated them from the room below. Peter could see shapes moving in it, and heard the grating of icy voices.

'It's a great hall,' he whispered. 'Like a throne room.'

Moke instantly came to life, and scuttled over to the window. Then he sat back, for once looking scared.

'Bad news,' he said. 'Bad, bad news. It's the Hall of Hagal himself, Lord of Storms. If he catches us, we're done for.'

As he spoke, the cloud gave a lurch down into the mist, and thunder rolled and throbbed up to them through the darkness.

6

Stargazers and Telkins

'Watch out!' hissed Moke, and scrambled back from the window.

Underneath, Peter saw a pair of yellow, glaring eyes, and a giant figure starting forward from a black throne.

'What's that?' demanded a booming voice, which sounded angry and fretful both at once.

'Doubtless another small explosion in the thunderworks, Your Excellency,' said another voice.

'Well, find who's to blame and have them punished,' snapped Hagal. 'We can't afford mistakes—not a single one. Not now.'

As Peter's eyes got used to the dark, he saw that the hall was filled with shadowy figures: looming storm-trolls, sky-courtiers, and generals, all dressed in shades of silver-grey or lightning-blue.

In the centre of the hall was a great table, and on it was spread a map.

'It's the Mainland,' Elsa whispered. 'What are they doing?'

The map was covered in markers, some shaped like clouds, others like whirlwinds or thunderbolts. The courtiers were leaning over the map intently, and sometimes a messenger ran in and whispered to one of them, and one of the markers was moved a little nearer the centre.

Hagal strode forward, rubbing his huge, icy-looking hands.

'Well, what news, what news?'

A storm-troll saluted. 'Two more thunderships moved up, Your Honour, and the hail squadrons and rain battalions are all in place. And all the storms have gathered. Last ones are just in: a long journey, sire, right over the Western Sea.'

Hagal rubbed his hands. 'Gathering nicely, nicely . . . Soon we'll strike, soon, yes . . . but what's *that*?' His finger jabbed at a single cloud-marker, sitting alone off the edge of the map. 'Do you mean to say we've had *losses*?'

'Just one hailcloud, sire, apparently crashed by accident. Hail goblin Slodkin commanding. Crew all picked up save one, still missing. No wreckage found.'

Hagal stared a moment at the crashed cloud symbol, and then he pointed an icy finger at the general. 'No slips!' he screeched. 'I'll have no slips! Our enemies are strong . . . All could fail . . . a single cloud, an *icicle*, could mean defeat . . . and has done, before now. Well? Where are the stargazers?'

Immediately a call went up, echoing through the hall so that the ceiling shook, and the stranded hailcloud sank shudderingly a fraction deeper into the mist.

'Stargazers!'

'Stargazers to His Majesty!'

Soon frosty feet were pattering on the hardened mist of the floor. Peter craned down, and saw a strange troop enter the hall. They were the creatures he had caught sight of before, peering from their towers: wise-looking, bearded cloud-beings, each with a telescope under one arm, and a tall, pointed, frosty-looking hat with strange signs scratched on it.

'Hail,' said the first, sweeping off his hat.

'We have come,' added the second.

'From the tallest tower: to unwind the wisdom of the stars, and make plain what the planets portend.'

Hagal came forward, with a look in his eye that was

part greedy, part fearful. 'Tell me, then,' he begged. 'What have you seen in the stars and the sky? Is the time right? I've got to win. Everything hangs on it. Mustn't make a slip—strike when the moment's right—not sooner, not later. Why should the others rule, and not me? Are they to win, without a war? I'll beat them. I must. Well? Did you see victory? Or defeat? Tell me! What?'

'We have seen, sire—'

But the stargazer got no further. His eye was drawn upwards, not to the stars, but to the widening gash in the ceiling, and the misty mass that was forcing its way gradually down into the hall.

'It's giving way!' shouted Elsa. The cloud lurched, throwing Peter away from the window. Moke leapt for the controls. In a moment he had jabbed the knob marked 'GO', and with a rending tear they crashed down through the mist and into the Hall of Storms.

'Yah boo to the courtiers!' shrilled Moke, as the cloud hit the floor with a jolt and bounced off. The storm-trolls growled with thunder and lunged after them, swatting and flailing, while the cloud darted this way and that like a trapped fly. Moke cursed away, swinging the levers and knobs round every time they nearly bumped into one of the walls. Hagal roared for his guards, and more and more cloud-creatures came pouring into the hall.

'Over there!' shouted Peter, pointing to a dark doorway set in the foggy wall. Moke steered straight at it, and now they were zooming along a corridor, with the trolls and courtiers still pounding along behind. Down shafts and stairwells they spun. Lightning glared from the dungeons where storm-giants worked, forging thunderbolts on anvils of ice; now one struck, now the next, pounding the sheets of fire with their fists. Then they were past, and on down an icy tunnel, where green light glittered from the snow-vaults.

'Where are you going?' yelled Peter.

'I know my way,' snarled Moke. 'Should be somewhere . . . ah!' He gave a furious twist to one of the crank-rods, and the cloud dived headlong down a twirling, spiral chute. The three of them spun screaming round and round, then shot out into the dull, grey daylight. A long way underneath the land was racing past, stony and featureless.

'What . . . was . . . that?' panted Peter, as the cloud stopped spinning and began to even out.

'Thunderchute,' gasped Moke. 'Where the lightning comes out. Spiral, to give it spin. Helps to grease it, too. Mind out!'

The cloud hit something with a bump, and Peter lost his balance. When he got to his feet, he saw they were jammed in a mass of other hailclouds like their own.

'Small fry!' shouted Moke out of the window, twirling and yanking and aiming a series of collisions at the clouds nearby. 'Why can't I have some room?'

The faces of other goblin pilots appeared at misty windows.

'Small fry yourself!'

'Look where you're going!'

'Skyhog!'

'Moke!' Peter shouted. 'Take us in to land, *please*! We're so near: the hermit—'

But Moke only jerked the controls back and threw them forward again, sending the cloud spinning off into another dive. The wind screamed, and the grey mountainside whirled up to meet them.

'What are you doing?' yelled Elsa. 'We're too low!'

'It's the cranks . . . some of 'em must've got busted . . . can't think how—'

In a moment, Moke was screaming along with the other two. They were hurtling down along the course of a stream, closer and closer, and then suddenly the ground dropped away, and they shot out over a waterfall. The cloud grazed its foaming lip, and then the din of the tumbling white water was behind them, and below was nothing: a bottomless drop between hanging ledges of rock.

'Look out!' shouted Moke. 'Ravine! Too narrow!'

They plunged down into the abyss, catching and bumping from rock to rock. A gnarled tree rose in front, the cloud tipped over and rolled down and down, with hailstones, ladle, children, and goblin tumbling over and over inside. At last they came to rest, wedged against a boulder with a stream pouring in through the cockpit and out of the hailchute behind.

Peter crawled to the door, staggered dizzily out on to the slope, and slipped and rolled down to the bottom. There he lay, dazed by the stillness, his head spinning. Elsa followed rather more steadily, and then Moke came plodding down to join them. Peter turned on him in fury.

'You utter *goblin*! You're *useless*! Why couldn't you land us, like we said?'

'It was all that hail-casting,' said Moke sulkily. 'Got carried away.'

'I suppose you think that's an apology,' put in Elsa. 'Well, it isn't!'

'You crashed us *again*!' Peter stormed. 'Three crashes in one day! And we were so *near*!'

'Well we won't be crashing it any more after this, worse luck,' Moke grunted. 'So *that* should please you.' He nodded at the melting, misty ruins of the hailcloud. There was a great gash down its middle, and the stream was spilling out in between. As Peter took it in his anger cooled.

'So what are we going to do about it? Isn't there some way of mending it? Patching it with some more mist, or something?'

Moke slumped down on the ground and shook his head. 'It's a write-off. See that tear? In a few minutes the water'll melt it all to bits.' He heaved a whistling sigh. 'We've had it.'

Elsa glared at him. 'Well, are you just going to sit there?'

'Better than casting hailstones,' Moke answered, and began to whistle tunelessly.

'All right,' said Peter. 'Let's just ignore him if he wants to sulk. Come on, we'll find somewhere to sit down and make a plan.'

He pulled Elsa away. Soon they were sitting on a rock by the stream eating some of Elsa's supply of sausage and cheese, squashed but still edible. Peter looked up. The sides of the ravine rose sheer on both sides, with trees, rocks, and ferns jutting out over their heads. Far, far above, the grey clouds still raced past.

'Gathering,' he murmured. 'Something terrible's going on, I know it. This is why we had all those gales: all the clouds and storms in the world, gathering together . . . and the sea and the Firefolk, too. And Hagal was talking of war . . .'

'Grandfather will know what it's all about,' said Elsa.

'But we've got to get there first. And we were right *above* him! All we had to do was land! Where are we now? Have you any idea?'

'We're in a ravine,' said Elsa. 'And we've got to get out of it.'

'I knew *that*,' Peter retorted. 'How?'

'We climb the cliffs. Or we find some other way out. Most valleys open out if you follow them down far enough. Come on.'

Still munching, Elsa led the way downstream, casting an expert eye up at the rocks as she went. At that moment, Moke reappeared.

46

'You weren't leaving me behind, were you? Me—a waif, an orphan, cut off from my own kind?'

'You're going to be *very* popular with your own kind when they catch up with you,' commented Peter, putting the last piece of cheese in his mouth. 'Come on, keep your eyes on these cliffs.'

Moke stared.

'What are you doing?'

'Eating, of course.'

'*Eating?*'

'Flesh and blood has to keep itself together somehow,' he replied, quoting his mother. 'Now *please* shut up.'

Moke only stared harder. 'Flesh and blood? Is *that* what you're made of? Sounds *disgusting*.'

'Well, what are you made of, then?'

'Cold air, obviously.'

'Thought you were made of cold water,' called Elsa from in front. 'It's what you keep pouring on everything. Now can we have some quiet while I look for a way up these cliffs?'

They plodded along in silence, Elsa and Peter gazing upwards, and Moke staring crossly at his feet. After a while, they stopped and exchanged startled looks. The ground had shaken beneath them.

'Is the land supposed to do that?' asked Peter.

'No. It's not.'

'Well, what does it mean?'

Elsa frowned. 'I don't know. Come on. The sooner we get out of this ravine the better.'

But ahead the cliffs only rose more steeply, and soon the ravine came to an end. They were standing on the brink of a cliff, overlooking a huge, misty valley. Beside them the stream shot out into the green abyss, the water floating down out of sight in a pattern of drops that was never the same, then drifting back up in a fine spray of mist. Peter stood and stared. He had never seen water do anything like that.

Elsa gave a grunt. 'Down there's the valley where we started, but we'll never get to it from here. Come on. We've just got to hope there's a way out at the upper end.'

They turned and climbed back up the ravine, past the tattered remains of their cloud. But soon afterwards they were once more forced to stop. Another waterfall pattered down from high above their heads, and just beyond it the valley came to an end in sheer rock walls. Elsa heaved a long sigh.

'I was afraid of that. We're in a hanging valley.'

'What's that?'

'It's one that's stuck on the side of the mountain, part way up, part way down, and no way out. We're trapped. Thanks to the *goblin*.'

Moke began to whistle innocently. Elsa gazed up again at the cliffs, but Peter stepped up to the dark, glistening rock around the waterfall. Something had caught his eye, a thickening among the shadows. As he clambered towards it, the thing only loomed darker and larger, and then he saw it was a cave. A breath of cold air fanned his face, and he drew back with a shudder.

Elsa was beside him.

'Now *that's* something like a find! How far in does it go?'

'I . . . I don't know,' Peter faltered. Elsa plunged past him into the crevice, and a few moments later she was back, smiling.

'There's a tunnel—goes right in. That's really luck!'

Peter hung back. 'You mean, go in there? In the dark? Under all that rock?'

'Why not? Under the mountain's as good as over.'

'But it might not even come out anywhere! You could wander for years!'

Elsa frowned at him. 'Look. That tunnel's man-made. Got to be: see how straight it goes? And whoever made it must have come from somewhere that isn't here, mustn't they? So all we have to do is follow it until we come out wherever it was they started from.'

'Who's "they"?' Peter asked.

'Miners, most likely. There's gold and silver all through these mountains. Come on! Mines always come out in more than one place, and they aren't built to get lost in. Have you got a better idea?'

Peter shook his head. The horror of the land was on him again: the vast, dry reaches of it, and the dark unknown places winding through its stony heart. But there was no choice. The Island, the village, his family and home, all depended on him.

'All right,' he agreed at last. 'We'll try it.'

'NO!'

Elsa and Peter spun round. It was Moke, sitting on a rock with his arms folded, wearing his fiercest frown.

'I won't go. Not underground. I refuse. Absolutely not.'

'No one's asking you to,' Peter snapped. 'Just sit where you are, and good riddance.'

'Well, you needn't think you're leaving me behind,' replied Moke, sounding deeply hurt. 'I'm going where you are!'

'In that case you must be coming underground,' said Peter. He faced up to the black opening, and swallowed his fear. 'Come on, Elsa.'

Moke slid off his rock and followed. 'It's not fair,' he grumbled. 'Tying a poor goblin in knots with clever talk.'

Peter clambered in past the spattering drops of the waterfall, and felt his way forward into the dark. Icy fear crept over him as the light dwindled behind: perhaps the last light he would ever see. And in the dark it would be easy to be separated, and wander on and on, alone until the end.

'We'd better hold hands,' he whispered.

'All right,' Elsa whispered back, and then let out a screech that echoed again and again from the walls of the tunnel.

'What's the matter?' Peter hissed.

'That . . . that . . . *goblin*!' Elsa spluttered. 'Its hands are like ice!'

'*Obviously*,' muttered Moke.

'Quiet, both of you,' whispered Peter, and the threesome advanced into the darkness, the only sound coming from the splashing of the waterfall and the muttered complaints of Moke.

'They're mad. It'll be dark. It'll be hot. I'll melt. We'll get lost.'

'Shut . . . up,' breathed Peter.

Step by step they moved along the passage. Peter groped ahead into the darkness with his hand in front of his face. The light from behind disappeared completely, and still the passage carried on, silent and eerie, blacker than night. After what seemed like forever he paused. Up ahead was a faint, pale dimming in the darkness.

'What is it?' whispered Elsa.

Peter swallowed. 'I think I can see light up ahead.' It was what he had been longing for, but now that he saw it he was afraid.

'Well, keep going,' Elsa urged. 'Let's see what it is.'

They crept forward. Soon the light grew bright enough to see by, and then they came out into a wide cavern. Jagged shadows jumped across its floor. A good way off, beside the far wall of the cave, a parade of drab-looking creatures was marching by, their grey heads cast down, their long, brown-clad arms swinging. Each one carried a smoking torch.

'What are *they*?' whispered Peter.

'Those are telkins,' answered Elsa: 'delvers—Earthfolk. They live in the ground.'

The last of the column passed by, and darkness slowly returned.

'Are they . . . dangerous?' asked Peter.

Elsa didn't reply. After a moment she said, 'Might be an idea to follow them, though. We've no light. And if we're in *their* country, and not just a mine . . .'

Peter jumped. 'Listen!'

Faint sounds were all around them: crackling, scrabbling, pattering sorts of sounds, like the legs of insects scratching on rock. Terror seized them, and then Peter felt himself grabbed by strong arms.

7

The Labyrinth

Darkness pressed against Peter's eyes, and cold air blew around his face. He was being jolted along through a tunnel, now on the flat, now climbing steeply upwards. From all round came the horrible sound of scrabbling, tapping legs. Apart from that he could hear only his own hissing breath, and of course the loud complaints of Moke.

'I'll fight you! I'm stronger than you'd think! You'd better let me go! You're in dead trouble, I'm telling you!'

But he soon grew tired, and they were carried on into the mountain in silence. After what seemed like hours, a faint glimmer of light returned, and Peter shuddered at what he saw. He was mounted on a broad, shiny back between two silent telkins. Ahead waved a pair of probing feelers, and all round him were pale, gleaming eyes, belonging to horrific, leggy creatures. By his side a giant wriggling centipede pattered along, scuttling on the rock with thousands of scratchy claws; beyond it a great slug-like beast was rippling noiselessly over the ground, its single foot flexing under its slimy body. Then there were others, leathery, stalking bat-creatures with tiny bodies and long, striding legs; dun-coloured toads with golden eyes; silvery beetles with rows of earth people seated on their backs, like the one Peter himself was travelling on. He closed his eyes, but the scuttling, padding, hopping sounds brought the sight back to him, and he opened them again with a shiver.

They entered a wider tunnel, lined with torches, and

passed through a high gateway. Dimly-seen creatures squatted in the shadows on either side, watching malevolently. The motley band scrabbled and hopped and jumped to a halt, and went on fidgeting while Peter, Elsa, and Moke were let down on to the ground.

Peter staggered a few paces and was held back by some leering, bearded troll-creature with a mace. He stared round in horror. All round him were dusty, cobwebby underground things. He shivered, and just for a moment home came into his mind: home and the sea, clear, cool, and wide, under an open sea-fresh sky. He shook his head to put the thought away. It was no use being homesick. He forced himself to concentrate on where he was, and see if there was any chance of escape.

They were in a great hall, thronged with telkins. Some of them were talking in whispers, but most kept a respectful silence, and were peering at the far end of the hall. Peter followed their gaze. The further down the hall he looked, the more ornate were the telkins' costumes, and beside each group was some sort of chamberlain or official. The one closest to Peter had a wooden staff, and was dressed in a brownish sack-like material, but the next one along had a staff of iron, and a silver-grey robe like a cobweb. Beyond that they sported great top-heavy headdresses and flapping collars with lashings of braid and lace; but all their costumes were dusty and faded. The last one of all had an enormous three-pointed hat, and a reddish robe that flowed down over the floor. He carried a great crystal staff which was obviously far too heavy for him to lift by himself: it was actually being held up by a troll-like creature standing behind, its hairy arm reaching over the telkin's head.

Beyond the last chamberlain there was a throne, made of gold and silver melted and poured together like a waterfall frozen in place. On the throne sat an elderly woman, and as soon as Peter saw her he began to be really afraid. Deeply pitted eyes gazed coldly over the hall as her grey, wrinkled face turned slowly from side to side. Her hair was white, and her dark, rustling dress sparkled with dusty jewels. She looked cruel as stone, and older than the mountains.

The ancient queen raised a pair of cloudy-looking spectacles to her eyes, and whispered to the chamberlain. At once he began heaving at his staff. The troll behind him noticed, and obligingly lifted the great rod of crystal and brought it down on the ground with a thunderous clang. The next chamberlain immediately struck the floor with his own staff of dusty gold, the one after did the same with his of blackened silver, and so it went on down the line, bronze, tin, brass, and iron, until the last chamberlain of all thumped his wooden staff in front of Peter's captors.

'Bow and be humble!' bawled the chamberlain. 'For you are before Geraia, Queen of the Earth!'

The crawly, scrabbly mass of beasts behind Peter subsided obediently, and the whole hall was silent. Then a hollow, booming voice rang out through the cave: it was the chamberlain closest to the throne.

'Your Majesty's legions have gathered,' intoned the telkin, shaking out a long roll of parchment. 'Trond, lord of the trolls . . . ' A hulking figure bowed sombrely from the shadows, together with a shaggy band of evil-looking followers.

'The boggles and the gettles . . . ' First, a mob of squashy, long-armed creatures halfway up the hall began to curtsy and caper, and then, at the mention of gettles, all the leggy, scuttly things round Peter hopped and shifted and were silent.

'The slow-worms and the telkins, with all Your Majesty's wise men, magicians, and sorcerors.' The chamberlain rolled up his scroll, as each group bowed in turn, ending with a gaudily-dressed clutch of figures next to the throne, armed with an assortment of wands and books and instruments. They grinned and bobbed, and swept their trailing, floppy hats on and off so many times that the chamberlain coughed to make them stop.

'That is good,' grated the stony voice of the Queen. 'We shall march together to the Summons, and our long exile will come to an end.'

The telkins and trolls, worms and boggles and gettles roared and thumped and shifted and scratched, each in its own fashion, until Geraia raised her grey hand, and they all fell silent.

'Banished to dust and darkness,' hissed the voice. 'Our honour lost, our legions smashed, ourselves betrayed . . . and all by our Mother's malice and the treachery of our sister and brothers. Holla would have had us hold back, and Hagal and Brand would have fought us . . . but a day will come . . . a day for revenge . . . '

Her voice crept on, cold and quiet and slow. There was a horrible, stubborn strength in it, and a rage which Peter felt could break rocks and overturn mountains if once it was let loose. He shivered, and Geraia's hissing voice slid through the silence like a snake.

'A day for vengeance, and the rising of the rocks from their still sleep . . . our rightful inheritance, stolen and wasted . . . banished to dust . . . robbed, betrayed . . . '

Just then a breathless telkin ran into the hall, skidded to a halt before the frowning chamberlain with the wooden staff, bowed and whispered something in his ear. Then the chamberlain bowed back, turned stiffly and approached the next official up the line, bowed and whispered. So the message passed up and up, until at last it came to the telkin with the great crystal staff, who bowed, turned to the Queen, and coughed, ever so quietly. Geraia's eyes snapped towards him, and the tirade ceased.

'Well?'

'If it pleases Your Majesty, a messenger has come.'

Geraia nodded, and now the chamberlains began their bowing again, all the way down the line. The last one motioned with his wooden staff, and the messenger, still panting, sprinted forward into the hall.

'The Firefolk, Your Majesty! Broken deeper in! Our sentinels—beaten back!'

Geraia brought her hand down on the arm of her throne; softly, it seemed, but the ground shook. 'Again the Firefolk! Where? How far? Show us!'

The court was in commotion. Several of the Queen's wise men bustled forward, bringing with them a huge thing like a three-dimensional spider's web made of threads of gold, with jewels hanging in the glittering mesh like flies. The messenger darted forward and began pointing at this jewel and that.

'They've reached the Long Chamber, Your Majesty, past the Painted Gallery; through the Cave of Bones and the Room of Voices—almost as far as the Labyrinth!'

The gettles were shifting uneasily, and Peter had managed to edge closer to Elsa. 'It's a map,' he whispered, and she nodded, her eyes fixed on the end of the hall.

Then with a deep murmuring grumble, the ground began once more to shake. Peter looked up: Geraia was trembling with rage.

'Am not *I* the one whom Destiny summons? And would Brand's children steal the honour that belongs to us? *We* are the eldest born of Night. The inheritance of the world is ours!'

The courtiers roared their praise, and the trolls began to beat their drums. The earth shook with a rumbling growl, the chamberlains hammered their staffs on the ground, and all were crying out, 'War! War! War!'

'Brand will be chained under a hundred mountains,'

Geraia raged. 'We shall bury the fire and bury the sea! Pile mountain on mountain, and crag on crag! Snatch sun and stars and clouds from the skies and tomb them a thousand leagues below ground. Then *I* shall reign! I alone!'

The drums boomed, the telkins roared, and the gettles scuttled on the shuddering ground. Geraia's voice dropped to a hiss.

'Destiny calls us. Even now I hear its voice, drawing us from our exile, beckoning us to the dominion of the world. "Come," it whispers, "come!"'

At the last words, Peter's heart seemed to go tight within him. He looked from left to right. His guards were paying him no attention, their eyes fixed on the raging figure on her throne. Peter ran forward, out into the middle of the hall.

'It's not true!' he shouted, and at once Geraia's cold eye was upon him. 'It isn't just you: everyone's been summoned. Holla can hear the voice too, but she's keeping back. You've got to hold out against it, or something terrible will happen!'

He gazed around at the faces of the chamberlains, who looked so shocked by his breach of etiquette that they had no idea what to do. But the ground still shook, the drums still thudded, and Geraia was staring at him, quivering with rage.

'What . . . thing . . . is . . . this?' she mouthed.

The chamberlains exchanged helpless glances, and then the wise men and magicians rushed forward in a body and clustered round him, measuring him with rulers, peering at him through spectacles and telescopes, and scribbling their theories in books. But the oldest and wisest-looking ones hardly glanced at him, and began drawing queer signs on the ground, and throwing down strangely marked pebbles and bones, which they gathered up, read, and threw down again. After a few moments the oldest of the sorcerors turned to the Queen with a helpless shrug.

'A thing beyond our wisdom, Your Majesty—a thing of the open air.'

'A dream, Your Majesty,' put in a second. 'A freak, a whim: a thing from away and beyond.'

'An oddity,' a third agreed. 'An idle thought in the maker's mind. Pay no attention to it.'

'No! You must listen!' Peter tried to shake off the clinging crowd of telkins, while Elsa broke free from the gettles and ran to join him, with Moke trailing after her.

'Spies!' Geraia mouthed. 'Spies sent from Holla! Tricking sneaks, earth-things that love the sea, and traitors to me, your rightful Queen!'

'I'm no subject of yours,' Peter retorted, but Geraia let out a hiss of rage and stretched her bony finger to point at him. Peter fell back over the trembling ground.

'You're *mine*!' rasped Geraia. '*I* shall rule! Not Holla, nor Hagal, nor Brand! Take them away! Let them lodge in the deepest dungeon, below the mountain's root. Things live there that have never seen the light since the world began. *You* will forget it too, in time, and learn to know your Queen!'

Earthfolk sprang forward and seized Peter and Elsa by the arms. They struggled helplessly, but at that moment another messenger rushed in, and spoke just two words.

'The enemy!'

At once, all was confusion. The wise men bundled up their instruments and snatched away the golden map, trolls stampeded forward with Trond at their head, roaring their war-cries, and chamberlains hitched up their robes and darted out from underfoot as best they could. Fire glared on the walls. Great dancing shadows shot to the ceiling, showing the warring silhouettes of serpents and

'Right.' They heard Moke scramble to his feet and patter off down one of the passages. 'Come on, then.'

'Wait! Where are you going?'

Moke's voice echoed hollowly from ahead. 'I'm made of air, remember? Fresh air, sky air. And I think I can smell my way back to it a bit better than *you* with your "flesh and blood", and "eating", and other foolishness.' He gave them a derisory sniff, and trotted off along the tunnel. Peter and Elsa ran to catch up.

Moke led them this way and that, winding and turning, but always tending upwards. The darkness was complete. From time to time the ground still shook, but the noise of fighting grew fainter. Then light gradually returned, and they came out into an enormous cave.

Peter let out his breath in wonder. Before them was a line of miniature volcanoes, with flames flickering from their smoking vents. Waves of heat hit them, and shadows danced up the walls in the fitful glare of the fire.

Moke sniffed the air and scowled.

'Which way now?' asked Elsa.

'There,' growled Moke. 'Past the fires, and up. Freeze it! We'll have to hurry, and hope.'

He led them jogging along, across the floor of the giant cavern. Steam hissed from the volcanoes, and smoke billowed out with a gentle 'Aah!' like the breathing of a giant asleep. Moke was going more slowly now, and kept stopping to heave enormous yawns.

'What's wrong with you?' Elsa demanded. 'Keep going!'

'Can't . . . can't help it,' yawned Moke. 'This heat . . . makes me sleepy. Just shake me if I slow down.'

In another few steps Moke fell snoring against a rock, and Elsa began shaking him and shouting in his pointed, frosty ear.

'Wake up. Wake up!' She turned to Peter. 'It's hopeless! Give me a hand, can't you?'

But Peter was staring at the closest of the fires, fascinated. This one was larger than the others, and wasn't shaped like a volcano. It was a gaping pit of heat, with fire and steam swirling and shimmering from it in a warm, sleepy rhythm. He drew nearer and nearer to the edge, and peered down into the flames.

Deep, deep below, fiery shapes seemed to be moving, drawing together, gathering into definite form. Perhaps this was the very fire into which Brand gazed, and from which he drew his wisdom; and perhaps if Peter stared into it long enough, he might grasp it too.

'Hey!' It was Elsa. 'Not you too! You can't *both* go into trances! Come away!'

The shapes were still gathering; in a moment the flames would form into signs and symbols, and the secrets of the fire would be his. But then the heat surged against Peter's face, and flames leapt up, high as the roof. Fiery shapes came rushing from the depths and began to hop clear of the pit.

'Run!' shouted Elsa. She snatched Peter back from the fire, and caught hold of the dozing Moke by one arm.

'What? What?' Moke shook himself awake, glanced back, and let out a whistling shriek. Then he was running ahead of them over the rocks, up the rising slope towards the far wall of the cave.

Peter stumbled and glanced back. The earth was trembling again, and behind them the Creatures of Fire were swarming up from the craters, column after column. First were the captains, riding on shimmering salamanders and fire-serpents, then the fire goblins, arrayed for battle, their spears and armour white-hot, their flame-coloured banners waving in the steamy air. The army surged towards them with a wave of heat, and began to climb the slope.

'Faster!' shouted Peter. But Moke had begun to slow down, and in a moment more he had stumbled to the ground again, and lay there snoring like thunder.

'Wake up! Wake up, you . . . you goblin!' Elsa prodded and kicked, but Peter was gazing uphill in horror. The lip of the slope seemed to be rising upwards, like a cliff ready to fall.

'Behind that boulder!' yelled Peter. 'Quickly!' Together they dragged Moke to safety, and then down like a fall of rocks came rumbling the army of the Earthfolk. Drums thundered, the ground quaked, and the vanguards of the two armies met head on. Banners of brown and grey mixed with yellow and red. Trolls stood out against the flames, swinging their clubs among the Firefolk, while gettles scurried forward, and golden nets flew from the hands of the telkins mounted on their backs. Some of the Firefolk were caught, but others burned their way free and came shrieking on, whirling their curving, fiery swords against the clubs of the trolls.

Crouching beside their rock, Peter and Elsa delivered the snoring Moke a series of furious pinches and prods. At last the goblin stirred.

'What? What is it?' He stared round at the burning, fighting figures. 'Ugh! Keep 'em off! I'll be evaporated! Take me away from here!'

'*You* were supposed to be taking *us* away,' Elsa reminded him.

'Well? It wasn't *my* fault. I'm a hail goblin, not a battle goblin. I can't smell battles.'

'Calm down,' Peter hissed. 'Can't you two ever stop quarrelling?' A rattling earwig-like creature scuttled past, spurred on by a whooping telkin, who aimed his lance into a cluster of Firefolk. Peter turned back to Moke. 'How far is it?'

Moke sniffed the breeze thoughtfully. 'Oh, not *far*, if

we can get out of this lot. It's just up there, where the Firefolk were heading.'

'Or where the Summons was calling them,' corrected Elsa.

'All right,' said Peter. 'We watch for a gap, and then we run. And *don't* fall asleep.'

A band of Firefolk charged by, beaten back a moment later by some trolls, who came storming down the hillside, shaking the earth with their footfalls.

'Now!' shouted Peter. Elsa gave the snoozing Moke a vicious prod, and they rushed out from behind their rock. Bodies of telkins lay thick on the ground, together with the smouldering ashes of the slain fire goblins. But the battle was moving further off, and they had only to dodge a fleeing group of riderless gettles before they were out of the cave. They ran on in the dark up a steeply climbing passage, and soon Moke showed signs of reviving.

'Ah! Can't you smell it? Snow! Cold! Storms in the high mountains!'

A moment later they burst from the tunnel and stood in the open air. It was dusk. A freezing wind was howling over the mountainside, bringing spatters of stinging rain.

'Beautiful!' murmured Moke.

Peter pulled his mantle round his shoulders.

'I only hope you've some idea where we are,' he murmured to Elsa. 'Because something terrible is happening. Something really, really terrible.'

Elsa had been casting her eyes over the rocks and hills in a knowing manner. 'Well, we'll learn all about it soon. I see where we are all right. Home's just up ahead. Grandfather will know.'

9

Birchbark and Chimneysoot

Elsa led them forward between rocks and boulders, and the odd patch of snow, bright in the twilight. Soon Peter heard the sound of a stream from ahead.

'Not far now!' Elsa called back.

Suddenly there was a harsh animal cry, and Peter saw a crowd of ghostly shapes coming trotting towards them through the rain.

'It's more of them! Run!'

Elsa chuckled.

'Good old Billy! I knew you'd be all right.' She turned to Peter. 'Oh, come on! You're not *still* afraid of goats?'

Peter let out his breath, and followed Elsa, feeling shaken and rather foolish. She led him to the brink of the stream where it divided in two, roaring around a great black rock in the middle. Spray rose into the air, and ferns clung to the dank stone. Peter realized this must have been the thing they had seen from the air, and which Elsa had pointed to as Grandfather's house. Close to, it still looked just like a rock.

'There we are!' Elsa said. 'Home!'

'I don't see anything.'

'You're not meant to.'

'Well, where's the house, then?'

'Up there. Jump!'

Elsa leapt across the churning water to a slippery-looking ledge, greasy and shining in the rain, and then made her way up a series of steps cut in the rockface. Peter looked down once, and swallowed. It was water, but how unlike the friendly sea at home! This water was shallow and cruel, murmuring angrily from where it ran trapped by the stones of the land. But it would reach the sea in the end . . .

'Hurry up!' Elsa called from above. Peter stopped thinking and jumped. He sprinted straight up the steps to join her, while Moke landed behind him with a clatter, like a large hailstone.

At the top of the steps, Peter found the boulder had a broad dip in it. In that dip was built a house, as black as the rock around it, and roofed with thick slabs of dark shale.

'Up here in the mountains it's wisest not to be seen,' Elsa explained. 'Come on.'

She went down a few steps and led Peter through a door. Inside, the house consisted of a single, round room. The chinks in the rough stone walls were plugged with moss, and windows made of woven lattice let in a glimmer of light. Across the room, a wiry-looking old man sat hunched at a desk beside the fire. He was scratching on a scroll of bark with a quill pen, while a second pen rested behind his left ear, and two pots of ink stood by his elbow. He had untidy white hair, and huge black eyebrows that crawled up and down his forehead as he wrote, like a pair of furry caterpillars. Peter had only a moment to look around in wonder before Elsa led him forward.

'No, no, no, wrong, wrong, wrong,' mumbled the old man as they came nearer. He scratched his long nose, tucked the pen he was using behind his right ear and took the other down from his left, and began making angry jottings on a second piece of bark stitched to the first. Then his eyebrows shot up, and the angry look vanished. 'Well, *could* be,' he muttered, and went back to his first pen and the other page. Elsa coughed, loudly.

The old man looked up, and his two scrolls rolled themselves up with a crackle. He stared at them.

'This is Peter,' Elsa said, pulling him forward by the sleeve. 'Oh, and that's Moke,' she added, nodding rather reluctantly at the hail goblin.

'Peter . . . Moke . . . ' repeated the old man, scribbling the names on a piece of bark. He stared at them again, and his eyebrows quivered. '*Now* I see! They're *visitors*, Granddaughter! Well, come in, come in, you and your little brother too, and sit by the fire. If only you had warned me, Granddaughter, I could have had some questions ready.'

Peter stepped forward, while Moke's eyes almost popped out with indignation. '*Fire?*' he spluttered. '*Little brother?* I'm off outside, I am, to sit in the cool.'

He stalked back outside, slamming the door behind him. There was an awkward silence. Elsa gave Peter a nudge.

'Peter's come from the sea. From an island.'

Suddenly the old man's eyebrows made a terrific plunge down over his eyes, and he leant forward keenly.

'An island! Land encircled by sea! That's it, isn't it?'

Peter nodded.

'The sea!' breathed the old man excitedly, and began digging through a pile of scrolls on the floor. 'Now perhaps,' he grunted, 'you can satisfy my curiosity . . . on a number of points. I have longed to travel, but no time, no time! So much to think, so much to write!'

Elsa meanwhile was steering Peter towards the fire and peeling off his soaking mantle. Peter stared back at the figure of Grandfather, who was reading from a piece of bark.

'Now, I have a book here which claims there are fishes in the sea with the faces of donkeys. What would *your* opinion be?'

'I . . . I've never seen a donkey,' said Peter. 'So I don't know.' He cast a bewildered look at Elsa, who was hanging a heavy pot over the fire. She took up a wooden spoon and began to stir it.

'Don't worry about Grandfather,' she whispered. 'It's his way of making friends, sort of.'

'And whales,' went on Grandfather, writing as he spoke. 'The same book maintains there are whales in the sea many leagues long, with forests and gardens on their backs.'

'I've never seen any like that,' faltered Peter. He was hoping to himself that this hermit was as good at answers as he was at questions.

'But there *might* be whales which accord with that description?'

'There could be,' admitted Peter, and Grandfather went on writing and muttering, 'Evidence . . . does not . . . rule out . . . '

'Grandfather's terribly clever,' Elsa whispered. 'He has all sorts of theories about how things work. He writes them all down in books, and then when he changes his mind he writes them down again. He's got a whole library— every word written by himself. He never needs to see anyone else. He can argue with himself quite happily. He never gets bored.'

She nudged a pile of curling birchbark with her foot. 'See that? That's what he makes his books out of.'

'He *makes* books too?'

'Makes 'em and writes 'em. Sometimes he even reads 'em.' She picked up a piece of the bark. 'You see how it's white on one side and brown on the other? Well, he uses black ink for the white side and white ink for the brown. I help with the ink. You make the black by mixing nut oil and chimneysoot. Sometimes the two sides of a page get into dreadful arguments with each other.'

'What's the white ink made from?'

Elsa gave him a queer look. 'You don't *really* want to know. Let's just say it's something birds leave on rocks. I let him gather *that* himself.'

She handed Peter a steaming bowl of stew and a wooden spoon, and began to ladle out a second bowlful.

'Will you be having supper tonight, Grandfather?'

The old man looked up suddenly, as if he had only just noticed Elsa's existence. 'Granddaughter! Now tell me, what is the state of the mountain?' He fished about for another piece of bark, and waited, pen poised. 'In as few words as possible, as I taught you.'

'Witchety,' replied Elsa. 'Herdhootslithery, flitflapping with gobhorrible groanowls, and allpathburntmonstrous trolltrodden.'

'I see, I see,' said Grandfather in a tone of great seriousness, and began writing furiously. Peter stared, his spoon stuck in mid-air. Elsa sat down beside him and began on the bowl of stew she had poured for Grandfather.

'It's just Grandfather's way of saving time,' she explained. 'If I'd said the mountains are all fidgeting with witches, slithering with horrible groany hobgoblins and herds of flapping hoot-owls, and the paths all trodden and burnt with trolls and monsters, it would have taken all day. What he really wants to do is to find just one word that means everything. Then you'd only have to say it once, and no one would ever need to speak again.'

Peter opened his mouth in confusion, and Grandfather spoke again.

'The *Igneus Populus*,' he intoned. 'Or, as the vulgar would say, the fire goblins or Firefolk. They are oozing up through the veins of the earth. But why?' He fixed them with a stern look, and all at once Peter's mind went back to the gathering of the sea, and the warring of Earth, Fire, and Storm. Fear struck him. It was time to ask his question, and the fate of his home depended on the wise man's answer.

'Please,' he began, 'the same thing's happening to the sea, or something like it. There's a voice that whispers, calling things together . . . Please, I was sent to find a Reprieve from the Summons.'

He held his breath, and Grandfather's eyebrows went up and then down. He leant back in his chair, repeating Peter's words over and over. Then he hunched forward and wrote them down.

'A *Reprieve* . . . from the Summons . . . a Reprieve from the *Summons* . . . ' He seemed to lose himself in thought, and sat for a long time staring into the gathering darkness of the room. Peter and Elsa watched him intently, and at last Elsa coughed. Grandfather started.

'What did you say?' He looked down at the writing in front of him. 'Yes, that was it: a Reprieve from the Summons.' Then he gave Peter a troubled look. 'What Reprieve? What Summons?'

Peter hung his head dejectedly. No one could help him. It would be the death of the sea—and perhaps something worse. 'I don't know. No one does. Holla said that some wisdom was needed beyond that of the sea. Over and away beyond, she said. She said you were wise—that you knew everything.'

Grandfather sank back in his chair. 'Ah, young man, I am not wise. Very far from it.' He heaved a vast sigh, and fell silent. Peter turned to Elsa, puzzled.

'Have I bothered him?'

Elsa shook her head. 'It'll be all right. You'll see.'

'I must read and think,' said Grandfather at last. 'I may have written something on the subject at some time—or I may not. You see,' he went on, suddenly fixing Peter with his piercing dark eyes, 'that is the reason why

I write books. The human brain is only so big, and it has holes in it. Things leak out. Now, my brain is a large one, but even so it will only hold nine hundred and sixty-two thoughts at most. After that they start to spill. And on an average day I have seventy-four new ones. So you see the problem. If I didn't write books, all those thoughts would just ooze away and be lost.'

Peter nodded slowly. 'I see. So you don't remember what's in the books you've written?'

'Naturally not. If I could, there'd be no need to have written them.'

Elsa set down her empty bowl. 'Grandfather, why don't I take Peter round the library himself? Then he can see if there's anything of use.'

'Yes, do, do, yes, by all means, Granddaughter. If there isn't, I shall just have to write something new on the subject. And before you go, Granddaughter, perhaps you would pour me a bowl of whatever it is I can smell. I think it may be stew.'

Elsa jumped up, handed Grandfather a bowlful of stew, and then turned to Peter. 'Dry now? Had enough to eat? Then I'll show you the library.'

They left Grandfather sipping thoughtfully at his stew, and Elsa led Peter across the room to a trapdoor in the floor. She heaved it up until it leant against the wall, and then Peter followed her down a flight of steps into the darkness.

10

The Book of Endings

'Grandfather doesn't allow candles in his library,' Elsa explained, as Peter followed her echoing footsteps, feeling along the wall to stop himself from stumbling. 'Too dangerous. Have you ever seen the way birchbark burns?'

'How do you see to read, then?' asked Peter, who was quite ready to be told that you didn't.

'Don't worry so!' Elsa laughed back. 'You'll see.'

They had reached the bottom of the stairs. They were in a dimly lit room the same size and shape as the one above, but this one was hollowed out of the heart of the huge boulder on which Grandfather's house was built. Up ahead there was a small window, from which Peter could hear the sound of the stream as it poured down over the rocks. As his eyes got used to the dark, he realized the room was packed with trunks and shelves and boxes and barrels, and all of them were stuffed full of crinkly birchbark books. He moved forward, and then turned to Elsa in dismay.

'There are no signs or labels! How do you find anything?'

'You look for something else. Grandfather says if you could find what you were looking for too easily, you'd never find the things you *weren't* looking for, and they're usually more important. Just plunge in: you'll soon find your way.'

Peter strayed off into the library. First he walked all round it. There were four windows, North and South looking out over the falls that rushed round either side of the rock, East facing up the valley, and West looking over a still pool, downstream towards the sea. The only part of the library that was empty of books was a single shelf in the very middle. Elsa appeared at his elbow.

'That's for Truth.'

'What?'

'The empty shelf: it's where Grandfather's going to put Truth when he finds it.'

'You mean he hasn't done?'

Elsa shook her head. 'He knows everything else; or at least he's thought everything, one time or another. But he's never found the Truth. That's why he won't let anyone call him wise. Come on: pick a book. Start looking.'

So Peter picked a book at random from a trunk standing beside the empty shelf. The cover was white, and it had written on it in black ink, *'Thoughts on Things*, volume 362'. He opened the book. The first page said, in white ink on brown, 'Telkins, gettles, and trolls all dig extensive tunnels underground.' Then an arrow pointed across to the facing page, which was written in black on white.

'Doubtless in order to discover the treasure of the earth,' said the writing. Another arrow took him back again.

'Preposterous. They already know where it is.' Then back to the other page.

'In that case, they are its guardians, and their tunnels are like the threads of a web, meant to trap the miners who go after it.' Another arrow.

'An ingenious theory,' the white on brown page replied. 'However, it is vulnerable to certain objections . . .' Peter skipped through to the end of the book, which finished with the advice, 'See *Concerning Troglodytes*, volume 96'. He dropped the book back in its trunk, beside *Typhoons and Tornadoes,* and *On Stormclouds and Those who Dwell in*

Them. He was beginning to see spots in front of his eyes. He pressed them shut for a moment, then moved on to another shelf, determined not to admit defeat.

The next book he found was called *Questions*. 'Why is water wet?' demanded the book. 'Why do rivers go downhill?' He leafed through page after page, wondering why only the brown pages had any writing on. Then he realized that all the books nearby were called *Questions* too. 'Why do people ask questions?' another of the books wondered, and then, as he got nearer the North Window, the books were filled simply with the word 'Why?' over and over and over. He put the last one back and closed his eyes again, feeling dizzy. Suddenly Elsa appeared beside him.

'How are you getting on?'

'Not very well,' Peter admitted. 'All these questions—they make my head spin. Look: this one says, "See *Doubts and Uncertainties*, third shelf from North Window". Maybe that'll help.'

'You don't want to go *anywhere* near that,' cautioned Elsa. 'You'll end up not thinking anything at all. If you go all the way north, you just come to blank books. Why don't you try the opposite side of the library? That's full of answers.'

Peter followed her southwards with relief. Soon they were both browsing among the Books of Answers, which had writing on the white pages and not the brown ones. Peter looked at Elsa in puzzlement.

'Are these the answers to the questions in the Books of Questions?'

'Of course.'

'Well, how do you match them up?'

'That's one of the things Grandfather spends most time on. He even wrote a book called *Which Questions Do Which Answers Answer?* That's one of the questions, of course. The answer to it's supposed to be somewhere among the Books of Answers, but he's never found it. Don't worry: come and look at this.'

She led him to the South Window, and handed him a book to look at. Peter leafed through it, but could make nothing of the contents. The book seemed to be full of disconnected words, not arranged in sentences.

'These are the Books of Words,' said Elsa. 'Grandfather moved on to them after he got fed up with Answers. I told you he was looking for the One Word that Says It All. Well, all the words in these books are his attempts to find it.'

Peter looked through several of them. Some of the words went on for page after page, all stuck together out of shorter ones; and some of them were nothing more than 'And', 'Because', and 'If'.

'Did he . . . did he find it?' asked Peter.

Elsa shook her head. 'No. It had a terrible effect on him. In the end he lost faith in the power of words altogether. For days he didn't speak, and the only books he wrote were full of blank pages. They went up by the North Window. Then he gradually worked his way out of it, first to Doubts and Uncertainties, then Questions. You see, he was moving south all the time, towards the centre. He was hoping that Questions would lead him to Truth, but just before he got to the middle of the library he changed direction.'

'Where did he go then?'

'He turned east. He started wondering where things came from; he kept probing and probing until he'd got to the East Window, and then he wrote the *Book of Origins*.'

'Where is it?' demanded Peter, suddenly urgent. 'I'd like to see it.'

'That's an easy one to find,' said Elsa. 'Last book under the window.'

Peter led the way, his heart beating fast. Soon he had the book in his hands, and began to read. The first chapter was headed, 'Chaotic Conglobulation of the Primal Elements. Separation of Seminal Matter'. He shook his head to clear it, read on, and gradually understood. 'It's about the creation of the world,' he announced. Elsa gazed back at him levelly.

'It says that at first everything was mixed up together. Everywhere there was a bit of light and a bit of dark, a bit of cold and a bit of hot. Nothing was any more one thing than another, so there weren't really any things at all. Do you understand that?'

'Traces of this and traces of that,' confirmed Elsa, 'mingling and separating, moving but standing still.'

'And then it changed,' Peter went on, frowning over the book. 'It says: "Then came Night, Mother of All. She drew the traces of things apart, giving each a being, separate from the rest. Four children she gave birth to: Geraia the eldest, earthy and stubborn; fiery-tempered Brand, stormy Hagal, and gentle Holla. And out of the traces she made a world, and made animals of all kinds to live in it, and lastly man. Then she left it all in the hands of her children, withdrawing into a cave above the ice on top of the world; and there she sat alone, sending her mind through the universe, and thinking on all she had done.

' "But before long the four Children of Night quarrelled. Geraia told them their Mother's day was done: Night, who ruled over chaos and dark, was banished, and now there was order and light. And who should rule the new world but she, Geraia, eldest born of Night?

' "But Brand said let *him* be the ruler: the strongest. And Hagal said yes, the strongest, but *he* was stronger than Brand, and he would fight him to prove it. Only Holla begged them to live in peace. But the other three took no notice of her, and went to war.

' "There were hurricanes and earthquakes, mountains shook and cities fell. But the Mother of All, alone in her dark cave, knew nothing of what was happening outside. The world would have ended when it had only just begun, except for an accident. In the Mother's cave, an icicle dropped, shaken loose by the earthquake. At the last moment of safety she rose up from her darkness, and saw the world on the edge of ruin.

' "Night towered in anger above her fighting children, and issued her decree. Never more would they roam free in her world. From then on they would live in banishment. Holla with her folk she sent to the seven seas, Geraia to the land beneath the earth, Brand to the fiery mountain, and Hagal she banished to the clouds, to wander the world, never resting.

' "And the Mother of All sits alone in the dark on top of the world, and her children are bound in their exile by a law that none can break. And the world is safe." '

Peter looked up from reading. A sense of horrible foreboding was growing on him.

'But they're *not* bound in their exile,' he murmured. 'They're leaving—gathering. Why? What's happening?' He looked down at the last page again. 'It says, "See rest of library". And then it says, "See *Endings*". What's that?'

Elsa looked up sharply. 'That's even worse than *Doubts and Uncertainties*. Why do you want it?'

'I don't know,' replied Peter slowly. 'I just do.'

'I told you the library was like that. Well, where do *you* think it would be?'

Peter looked across the library, its shadows deepening in the dusk. 'Far west,' he answered. 'Where the sun sets and the moon sets. Where things come to an end.'

Elsa nodded, and they turned back, past shelves of where this came from and how that started, past the empty place of Truth, and into the realms beyond. Peter moved slowly, examining the titles of books as he passed. 'Sadness,' he read. *'Melancholy Reflections, volume 66. Thoughts on Mortality.'* His forebodings grew the further west they went, until at last he was standing by the window that looked out over the still, quiet pool at the foot of the rock. He took the *Book of Endings* down from its shelf, his heart pounding.

'"When all things end . . . "' Peter read out. He stopped, licked his lips, which were suddenly dry, and went on. ' "When all things end, the sea will rise up and cover the land; fire will flow up through its cracks, and the mountains on the rim of the world will shower rocks into the sea. Storms and hail, fire and earth and sea, all things and all creatures will gather together. The Children of Night will make war, dreadful and deadly. Nothing will remain in its place, and nothing that is will be."'

Peter looked up, and read the final sentence, pale and trembling. ' "All this will happen when the elements are summoned together."' He stared at Elsa. 'Summoned! You see? All things and all creatures—the Children of Night and all their armies, gathering . . . '

They were silent for a moment. The darkness closed round them, and Peter put the book back on its shelf. It was growing too dark to read.

'Sounds like the family reunion from Hell,' murmured Elsa.

'Much worse than that,' Peter replied in a low voice. 'It's the end of the world.'

11
Plans by Firelight

Later that night, Peter and Elsa were sitting by the fire with Grandfather, having told him what they had read in the library.

'Origins,' mused Grandfather, 'and Endings. A most strange tale you have told me, Elsa. And is it really your opinion that I wrote these two volumes?'

'Must have done, Grandfather. *I* certainly didn't.'

He sighed and leant back in his chair.

'Now you'll hear something,' Elsa whispered to Peter. 'He's thinking about it.'

'A most strange matter altogether,' Grandfather resumed. 'When the four masters of the elements come together, they fight and destroy, but kept apart they make a world . . . One way war, the other beauty and order. Strange how the very same creatures can be the cause of opposite things . . . But then not so strange. That is the way some people are made. They're like fire and water: apart, both good. But together? Both die.'

Grandfather's eyebrows made a terrific plunge in the firelight, and the old man reached for a piece of bark and a pen.

'What are you doing, Grandfather?'

'Writing a book, Elsa. I shall call it *On the Fixity of Natures*. I think it will go just nor'-nor'-west of the centre—'

'Not now, Grandfather, or you'll forget what we're talking about.'

'But if I don't write the book at once, Granddaughter, I'll forget *that*.'

'I'll remind you. I promise. Now come on. The Summons.'

'The voice that whispers in their ears,' Peter prompted, 'calling out "Come, come". What is it? And why can the creatures of the four elements hear it, and not animals or people?'

Grandfather lowered his eyebrows and gazed at Peter intently. 'Perhaps whoever is issuing the summons has no use for animals and mankind. Perhaps whoever it is wants only the four Children of Night—them and their sundry minions.'

'But wasn't mankind made by Night?' Elsa asked. 'I thought she was mother of everything.'

'So, indeed, the Book of Origins claims, Granddaughter. But other books, which you did not find and which I have either never written or forgotten, might easily maintain that mankind was not created by Night at all, but someone quite else.'

'But the summons,' Peter insisted. 'Who's issuing it? And why? Why would anyone want to destroy the world? Don't they *know* what would happen?'

'An evil enchanter?' Elsa suggested. 'You do get them.'

'That,' said Grandfather, 'is one opinion. I have my theories, to be sure. Time will tell. Step by step, Granddaughter: we learn first one thing, then another . . . And I fancy "Who?" and "Why?" will be among the very last questions to be answered.'

'Go on, Grandfather. What questions *can* be answered?'

'For the moment, Granddaughter, I see just one thing clearly.'

'And what's that?' asked Peter. His head was beginning to spin again, and he was getting impatient.

'Just this: the world must be saved. For, while the end

of the world would probably not be the end of Truth, there's no doubt that it could seriously interfere with my search.'

Peter screwed his eyes shut. 'But *how* can we save the world, if you don't even know who's behind it all?'

'That,' said Grandfather, 'is easily answered. How to save the world! If only "What *is* the world?" could be answered as easily!' His eyes drifted off into the distance and his fingers twitched, as if he had scented Truth far off, and was itching to get back on its trail, and write another book.

'Carry on, Grandfather,' Elsa invited. 'Tell us what we have to do.'

Grandfather sighed, and drew his gaze back from infinity. 'The Mother of All, Granddaughter. She saved the world before, and she can save it again. She is the only being in the world, I take it, who has the power to send the four Children of Night back to their homes. But if you recollect, Granddaughter, on the last occasion it was only the falling of an icicle that rescued matters. That might not happen again. Someone'—And here he looked pointedly down at Peter and Elsa—'someone must make the journey to the top of the world, to the cave above the ice, and warn her. That, very simply, is what someone will have to do.'

Peter, gazing into the fire, nodded. 'I know,' he murmured. 'And I've come this far, so it had better be me. But it'll be dangerous. The fighting's already started.'

12
Travels without a Map

Peter woke next morning to the sound of the stream rushing over the stones, swollen by the night's rain. He sat up in his sleeping alcove, quickly pulled on his clothes, and drew back the curtain. Outside he saw Elsa packing things into a hairy goatskin bag, while her grandfather sat at his desk sucking one end of a quill, and regarding her with curiosity.

'Explain to me again, Granddaughter. Something appears to have escaped me.'

'I *told* you. I'm going with Peter to save the world. Oh, Grandfather, you can't have forgotten *already*. You've been up in the night, haven't you? How many books did you write?'

The old man held up his hands. 'Slowly, Elsa, slowly. Simply explain to me. In as few words as possible.'

Elsa sighed, and paused with a smoked sausage in her hand. 'We're on a treethingfolksaving rescuedash to the icefrozen worldtop, to staystop the dangerquake, and warsummoned allworld enddeath. That's what. It's in the library, Grandfather. *Book of Endings.*'

Grandfather's eyebrows did a plunge, and he began to write furiously. Peter got out of his alcove. Elsa turned in the act of stuffing cheeses into her bag and smiled.

'It's all right. He'll remember now.'

Peter looked at Elsa, and looked at her bag.

'You mean you're coming too?'

'Of course I'm coming. You don't think you could manage on your own, do you?'

'Why shouldn't I?'

'It's obvious. Look at you: you don't know what an owl is, or a goat, or anything. If I wanted to go to the sea, I'd ask *your* help. As it is, *you* need *me*.'

'What about your grandfather?'

'Oh, he'll be all right. Won't you, Grandfather? Just remember to milk the goats. And watch out for Old Billy. He butts.'

'Yes, Elsa,' replied Grandfather, writing scratchily. 'Milk goats . . . watch Old Billy . . . '

'You don't have to *milk* Old Billy,' Elsa explained. 'Only milk the nannies. That's very important, Grandfather. Do you think you can remember that?'

'Only . . . milk . . . the nannies. Yes, Elsa.' He finished writing and rolled up his book of bark. 'Now, I want you to make careful observations of everything you see. I've written you a Book of Questions to take along, and here's a pot of ink. Just write in the answers, Granddaughter. You understand me?'

'Yes, Grandfather.'

'Nice, simple answers—'

'Using as few words as possible,' finished Elsa.

'And if the world *should* come to an end—'

'Yes, Grandfather?'

'Be sure to write me a full description. You'll be in the very best position from which to observe it.'

Elsa sighed, and put the crumpled roll of bark in her bag. 'Well, I think that's everything. Food, warm clothing, book . . . Right then. Early start: breakfast later. All right?'

Peter nodded. Elsa shouldered her bag, and at the door she turned to look back. Peter saw her eyes glance over every detail of the room, which he knew she might be seeing for the last time. In the end her gaze rested for a long moment on Grandfather, and their eyes met. But all she said was:

'Only . . . milk . . . the nannies!'

Then she lifted the latch, and Peter followed her outside.

It was a cold, brilliant day. The clouds were gone; only the wind still whistled drearily in the heather. But as soon as they crossed the threshold the whistling stopped, and they saw Moke looking up at them.

'Just our luck,' Elsa grumbled. 'I was hoping he might have evaporated overnight.'

'Was that noise *you*?' asked Peter.

Moke nodded sadly. 'All night I've been calling to the clouds, and not one stopped for me. Oh, there's been all sorts going past: I've seen rain maidens and snow ghosts . . . hailclouds, too, all heading the same way they were, up into the mountains. Not exactly advancing in good order, but then they were late, and in a hurry. And now they're gone—all gone off to the battle. Biggest smash and crash in history, and *I* get left behind.'

'This is bad,' said Peter. 'If the clouds have all gathered, we haven't much time. Come on, quick. You just come with us. We're going the same way.' He ran down the steps cut in the rock and cleared the torrent in a bound. Elsa and Moke ran down after him.

'What did you have to *invite* him for?' complained Elsa. 'He's just trouble. Trouble the Goblin.'

'We can't just *leave* him,' Peter argued. 'Come on, we've got to hurry! Where do we go from here?'

'Well, up.'

'Up? I thought you knew the way!'

'Up's the theory. It's only putting it into practice that might be harder. *That's* why you need me.'

Peter looked round at the featureless mountains in despair. They were in a broad, grey valley, sweeping up all round them to chains of dark, broken peaks.

'Haven't you even got a *map*?'

'There *is* a chest of maps in the Library,' Elsa admitted, 'but I don't think they'd be much use.'

'Why not?'

'Well, they just don't match up with what's on the ground very well.'

'They're wrong, you mean.'

'Oh, no. The maps are right. Grandfather worked them out from first principles.'

'But then—'

'It's the *places* that are wrong. Grandfather's maps show how things *ought* to be, not how they are. The world's not a perfect place, you know.'

Peter squeezed his eyes shut.

'Don't you see we're beyond *theories*?' he shouted. 'We've got to *do* something! Move on, find a way, now, before the world ends!'

'*I'm* not holding us up—' Elsa began, when Moke interrupted.

'Quarrelsome pair, aren't you? Thought you two were in a hurry. The way's up here.'

Peter and Elsa ran to where Moke was standing. At his feet was a well-trodden path with every kind of footprint on it: webbed, clawed, three-toed, and burnt.

'You should have seen all the queer things that passed up here in the night. Hurrying, they were, all patters and slithers and gallops. Come on, can't you feel it?' Moke began to drift on up the path, a dreamy look on his face. ' "Come," it's calling. "Come . . ." '

Peter and Elsa looked at each other.

'Well?'

'Follow,' Peter replied. 'For the moment, it's all we can do.'

They ran after Moke, who was already a good way ahead, and moving surprisingly fast. As the path wound up and up out of the valley, Peter began to feel relieved. At least they were going up.

Before long they had left a last few stands of pine trees

behind them, and then they were climbing between barren crags, and trudging across snowfields and wandering rivers of scree. From time to time some strange creature overtook them: a riderless gettle, striding along on giant bird-feet, its batlike wings flapping; a troop of Firefolk, yellow banners streaming, scorching the rocks as they tore past; and then there were trolls and telkins, and other things that none of them could name. All of them came careering up the path in great haste, and disappeared over the brow of the slope.

When they came to the top of the rise, a new valley opened out, broader, greyer, colder.

'It's like the sea,' Peter said. But Elsa shivered.

'I don't like it. No trees, no cliffs . . . We might as well not *be* in the mountains.'

'Look!' Peter pointed. Far in the distance there was a brooding mass of cloud. Distant thunder boomed, and glints of lightning flashed between sky and ground. At the same moment they all felt the earth shake.

'Earth!' grumbled Moke. 'Nasty, dirty, wobbly place! When I think I could be up there, swooping, diving—'

'It isn't *normally* wobbly,' Elsa put in, but Moke cut her short with a hiss.

'Listen! It's calling again. Why can't you hear it? "Come," it says, "come . . ."' He drifted forward again, humming the words. They toiled on after him, over rock and snow. The further they went, the more easily Moke seemed to glide ahead over the ground, and the harder Peter and Elsa found it to keep up. And all the time the looming stormcloud drew nearer, like a lonely island in an empty sea. The sight made Peter think of his voyage with the Seafolk to the Cave of Holla. And how soon before she too was forced to obey, and the sea began to rise over the earth?

At last they crested a final rise, and then they stopped

and stared. Above them the blue sky came to an end, and after that there was only a churning mass of storm, with lightning flashing from cloud to cloud. Beneath lay a bleak, grey plain, with the everlasting ice beyond.

'There it is,' said Elsa. 'The top of the world.'

But they were not alone. Down on the plain, forces were on the move. Brand's army was breaking up through the ground on the left, casting a red glare on the clouds, and on a rocky hill to the right stood the stony, brown-bannered camp of the telkins. Gettles moved over the hillside, and the ranks of boulders massed on its brink were surely trolls.

'And the armies gathered,' murmured Peter. 'Right where *we* need to get through.'

As they watched, thunder shook the ground, and clouds boiled down over the mountain, blotting the armies from sight. The battle had begun.

13
The Top of the World

They hurried down the slope, and at once plunged into a bank of freezing, swirling mist. Hail beat against the rocks, and thunder rolled round the mountains. Rank upon rank of dimly seen clouds whirled past them.

'That'll show 'em!' yelled Moke. 'Look at those hailclouds! Perfect formation, swooping low, then pouring up over the Firefolk! You can even rain uphill in those light jobs—takes skill, though. The nasty sparkies didn't expect *that*!'

Sizzling cries came from over the brow of the hill, and reddish flares lit the murky sky.

'We'll never get through!' shouted Elsa.

'Just run!' Peter yelled back. 'We may as well be burnt or frozen or crushed right now as wait and have it happen to us later. Come *on*!'

Just then a sudden gust brought a cloud swerving in front of them. A goblin face appeared through the fog, and Moke skidded to a halt. The other two stumbled into him.

'Slodkin! Pick me up!'

The face scowled. 'So it's Moke, the champion cloud-crasher! You're in bad, bad trouble. Clatter says you'll be sent to count snowflakes for at least ten thousand years. Well? Coming?'

Moke's grin became a glower. 'Don't bother. I'm staying put. We've got important business, we have. We're saving the world.' He gave Slodkin a last venomous look, and turned to Peter and Elsa. 'Come on, you two. Stop dawdling.'

The cloud swept away. Hail and rain drummed round them; flames leapt from the hill, and then the clouds were rolling back again, the sun shone, and a heat haze shimmered over the army of the Firefolk.

'Mizzle and smite them!' cursed Moke. 'The attack's failed! But our lot'll be back! Never fear!'

They hurried under the base of the hill. Ahead loomed the glacier, glinting in the sun.

'Not far,' gasped Peter, as they toiled up the valley that separated the armies of Fire and Earth. 'We *will* make it.'

But at that moment blazing chariots shot from behind a spur of rock, drawn by steaming fire serpents. The chariots pulled up, blocking the way. Firefolk leapt to the ground and advanced on them menacingly. Peter glanced back. More Firefolk had climbed down from the ridge behind them and were moving up the valley.

'*Now* what?' asked Elsa. 'They've got us trapped.'

But suddenly the Firefolk stopped. They were gazing up at the sky, and their burning faces wore looks of horror. Above them, the clouds parted like smoke. A giant figure stood towering over the battlefield. His body seemed to be made all of whirlwinds and thunder, and he gazed down on the army of the Firefolk with contempt.

'Hagal,' murmured Moke with relish. 'Hagal has come!'

The next moment the ground began to tremble.

'The telkins!' cried Peter. He looked desperately for some way through the encircling ring of Firefolk, expecting the army of Earth to come rushing down on them at any moment.

But across on their hill, Geraia's army had not moved. The rumbling grew louder; then there was a wrenching, splitting, grinding jar, and above them the rocks of the hill were thrown apart. The Firefolk swept aside, and waves of heat beat down on them. A giant, fiery figure was slowly raising itself from the crest of the hill. On its head was a crown of burning gold; its scarlet hair blazed, and all its body rippled and flashed with flame.

'Brand! Brand!' chanted the Firefolk, while Moke tried to burrow under a rock, whimpering with fright. Then Hagal spoke from the clouds, with a voice like the hurricane.

'You summoned me, brother, and I came. Bad luck to you! Do you dare to start our old fight again? I'm the stronger. I was then, and am still. Luck's with *me*, whether the stars say it or not. Begone, back to your smoky den, before I destroy you! And take your sparks and cinders with you!'

Brand opened his searing, furnace-like mouth, and flames drove against the sky. 'It was *you* who summoned *me*! Treating your lord as if he were a slave! And I shall be the one to destroy *you*!'

Whirlwinds roared round the giant in the clouds, who stamped and kicked in fury, sending hailclouds and thunderbolts spinning aside.

'Do you dare? Do you still *dare* challenge me?'

'To the death!' roared Brand back. 'To the end of all things!'

'Very well!' threatened Hagal. 'Very well! First you, then her, and Holla last of all! I'll smash you all! The last fight, and the winner to rule forever!'

'I'll kindle your clouds and burn your sky! Fry your folk, and wither your pride to ashes!'

'I'll strike you down with a single bolt! I'll blast your fires to the winds!'

'Let it be so!' Brand bellowed back. 'Though the world perish! Burn, flames, and fires roar destruction!'

He threw back his head and let out a crackling roar of flame. Fire goblins swarmed from his throat, clinging among the hailclouds like sparks. Hagal answered with a rolling crash of thunder, and the clouds came sweeping down. Battalions of storm trolls trooped from the mist, their icy spears red in the fire's glare. The battle raged layer upon layer up into the sky. Flame snatched clouds from the sky, until foggy wrecks strewed the hillside. Banners advanced and retreated; Firefolk hissed and grew dim, and hail goblins flowed into water.

Peter peered out from behind their rock. Ahead, the fire chariots were deserted, doused and broken in the attack, and riderless fire serpents slithered away over the ground.

'Must . . . go on,' called Peter, over the roar of fire and storm. Elsa nodded. They hauled the terrified Moke out from his hiding place, and crept up the valley, round the edge of the battlefield.

'We're almost there!' Peter cried. The hill of the Firefolk was behind, and there before them lay the ice, spreading its giant grey fingers over the mountain. But close on their right sat the army of the telkins, their faded banners flying. And there in its midst was the dusty throne of Geraia, on a chariot drawn by many-legged gettles. Trumpets brayed, the trolls beat their drums, and the whole army began to rumble down off its hill.

'Hurry!' Elsa cried. 'They'll cut us off!'

They ran for the ice, slipping over the muddy ground that oozed from under the snout of the glacier. Drums thudded in their ears, and the earth shook to the march of Geraia's army. A rushing river of meltwater separated the telkins from the rest of the battle, but up ahead some trolls had lain themselves over it, forming a bridge, and the Earthfolk were beginning to cross.

'We're too late!' Peter yelled.

'One last try,' urged Elsa. 'Run!'

They scrambled forward up the muddy slope, and then they heard Moke's warning voice from behind.

'Look out: snow ghosts!'

A bank of cloud had broken away from the main body, and was whirling down on them. In a moment, blind whiteness blew all round. Peter could see nothing. He flailed about desperately, and caught Elsa's hand with his.

'Where's Moke?'

'Don't know. Come *on*!'

Then they heard his voice, receding into the blizzard.

'Leave off. I'm one of you. Go away, won't you? We can't see where we're going. Look, where's your chief?'

The snow whispered round them. A moment later the clouds blew clear; a powder of white lay on the ground, and Moke came trotting over to them, a wide smile on his face.

'Side attack! Clever! It's all right: they just didn't know whose side we were on. Look over there!'

Rain maidens were lashing the troll-bridge, sweeping chariots and telkins off into the river, while snow ghosts whirled round boggles and trolls, which swatted at them without effect. Chamberlains fled back up the hill, gathering up their robes in fright.

'Hooroar!' shouted Moke. 'That's the way to do it! See that rain? That's the real hard stuff. First they pass it through pipes to make it good and sharp, then they press it to squeeze all the warmth out. Next they mix it with ice and—'

'No time,' said Peter. 'Come on!'

They struggled up the last of the hill, and there was the ice, stretching towards them like a row of blue-grey claws. Between each claw was a gaping crevasse, reaching down to the ground to form a mysterious, dimly lit cave. Elsa and Moke vanished into one of the openings, and

Peter turned for a last look back. Thunder and earthquake merged with the troll-drums; over all the plain was a mingling of fire and rain, smoke and lightning and death. Peter turned away with a shudder, and slipped between two gleaming spires inside the ice.

Smooth, curving walls closed over him; ahead the tunnel wound on, lost in a blue, mysterious light. Water lay ankle-deep in the crevasse, while more water streamed down the glassy face of the ice, over swirls of bubbles trapped in its luminous depths. From above and below came the hollow rushing and whispering of unseen rivers, like the sound of many voices.

Peter splashed through the freezing water to catch up with the others. Moke was standing in front, drawing in great, snaffling breaths of fresh air.

'So there you are,' shivered Elsa. 'Hurry up, it's cold!'

'Wonderful, isn't it?' Moke agreed. 'Really something like home. Not that I wouldn't rather be in the clouds, mind, but this is the nicest place you've brought me to yet. Well? Coming?' He splashed off ahead, and Peter and Elsa followed.

The tunnel wound and narrowed, and then suddenly it opened out into a kind of clearing among a forest of pale, curling ice-columns. Everywhere they looked were swirling glasslike passages and hollow blue-glaring ice caves, which branched and branched again; and all round echoed the rushing of the meltwater, mingling with the distant din of battle.

'This is as bad as the labyrinth!' Peter burst out. '*Now* what?'

'And this time it's no use asking *him* to help,' said Elsa. 'All the air's fresh up here.'

But Moke ignored her. He had begun to drift off down one of the passages, and the dreamy look was back on his face again.

'It's calling . . . calling . . .'

'Moke!' Peter shouted.

'Let him go,' said Elsa. 'We'll try one of the others.'

'No! Don't you see? It's the Summons!'

Together they ran after him, slipping on the rounded spires of ice, and only just keeping the hail goblin in sight as he glided ahead through the maze. Pinnacles of ice rose round them, and gurgling torrents roared up from chasms at their feet; and still the passage branched and wound, and Moke glided on. And then the blue light dimmed, the ice walls fell back and they were on solid earth, with a great black crag before them, looming from the ice like an island in a frozen sea.

Straight in front of them a cave opened up. Moke had already drifted into it, and Peter and Elsa followed. And there in the darkness sat a great, throned figure, a lady robed in black, with a face as pale and gleaming as the moon. Her hands reached out to the mouth of the cave, beckoning.

'Come,' she was whispering, 'come.'

14

The Mother of All

Peter stood and stared. Before them, motionless in her black folds of drapery, sat Night, the Mother of All. Her hands were still raised, but her whispering had stopped, and she was gazing at her visitors questioningly.

Moke was the first to break the silence. He skipped suddenly forward, swept the pointed hat off his pointed head, and made a deep bow.

'Moke's the name, Your Majesty. A humble goblin, employed until recently on board one of Your Majesty's hailclouds.'

'And we're children,' Peter blurted out. 'Peter and Elsa.'

The staring moon-face crept into a smile.

'So! Two children and a goblin! The first of my creatures to come. But it begins. They are near. They have heard. My children will soon be with me.'

'And it was really you?' Peter demanded. *'Why?'*

'Why? To help me in the grand search: to help me find the Truth.'

Peter felt suddenly weak at the knees. He looked at Elsa, and back at the Mother of All, and he couldn't say a word.

'Truth!' whispered the Mother of All, and now she left her throne, and glided through the darkness of the cave like the moon sailing across the night. 'From the start of time I have looked for it. This world: I made it all, and knew it all . . . all but this one thing, Truth. And so I shut myself away, here in the dark, and began the search: the *great* search, for what in the world is of any weight beside Truth?'

Elsa was staring at her as hard as Peter. 'And you've been looking ever since? And you've still not found it?'

'They'll never help you,' Peter said.

The moon-face swept up close. 'But they will,' whispered the voice. 'They must. They're my last hope.'

Peter felt weak again, and this time he sank to the ground and sat staring blankly at the whisking moon-face, which darted through the shadows of the cave, now near, now far.

'For centuries I have searched,' Mother Night was saying. 'Thought after thought sprang into being in my mind, and I stored every one in the spaces of my intellect, brought it out, put it back, went round it and under it and through it. But when I had thought every thought there is to think, I had still not thought the Truth.

'Then I said to myself, the Truth is far away; my thoughts fall short, and cannot reach. So I began forging them together, linking thought to thought with rock-hard bonds of memory. At last I had it: the longest thought there is to think. It snaked away, far, far . . . It carried me off into strange, unimagined lands; but it didn't lead to the Truth.

'It took me years to get back, and for a long time my thinking was filled with the far-flung and the bizarre. At last my mind cleared, and then I thought: the Truth is above me. I have been searching too low. All I had to do was reach up, and it would be mine. So I took the links of my chain, and smashed them one from another. Then I heaped the thoughts into towers of notions on mounds of ideas, planted firm on deep-rooted principles, buttressed with side-thoughts, tottering with airy pinnacles of afterthoughts. Thought by thought I built it up, all cemented together by reasons and arguments. It was the highest, the hugest, the grandest thought there ever was. In my mind it took weeks just to walk round it, and years to climb. But it was no good. From the top I saw nothing but the tower, reaching up to me from below; and the tower wasn't Truth.'

Peter stared at her. He thought of the Mother of All alone in her world for long ages, building, making and unmaking, searching and beginning again, while outside the sun rose and set, and animals lived and died.

'What did you do then?'

'I stood back from my thought-mountain, and pulled it down. Thought split from thought, until the tower of my failure lay scattered round me in ruins. I came close then to despair. But soon my thoughts took a new turn. One of them whispered to me, "Truth is within," and at once I saw what to do. So I began to pull my ideas to pieces, looking for the hidden thought inside each, and then pulled that to bits too. But there was always something more, behind and apart, within, beyond my sight . . . And in the end I was left with nothing: vacant thoughts, cast aside and useless, and my mind was empty.

'For years after that I thought nothing at all. But then I began to have feelings, and from feelings I built up to notions, and then back to thoughts. And they were the same thoughts as ever: thoughts of this and thoughts of that, but never a one of them was Truth.'

'You *are* like Grandfather,' Elsa burst out. 'Don't you ever forget anything?'

'Never. My mind has no end. Not one thought has ever slipped from it.'

'That's why there are no books,' Peter muttered. 'And what then?'

The moon-face flitted back to its throne. 'Then I issued

the Summons. My wisdom was used up. Geraia was right, perhaps, and my day was done. But my children have wisdom of their own. Perhaps Holla has heard the Truth, singing to her in the voice of the sea, or Geraia learnt it from her pebbles and bones. Or Hagal may have seen it in the stars, or Brand read it in the heart of his fire. I have to know!'

They stared, and just then a faint murmur reached them from the distant battle. Peter jumped. The dreamy darkness of the cave had blotted out any thought of the world outside, just as it had through all those centuries for the Mother of All. He started towards the throne.

'But don't you *remember*? Before you sent your children into exile?'

The bright face clouded, and the Mother of All frowned.

'You *do* forget things! It was the end of the world—the battle to end all battles!'

'It seems I do remember something of the sort . . . ' the Mother of All reflected. 'Something from outside my mind. A sound, it was . . . a clatter, a tinkle . . . '

'It was an icicle,' Peter pressed her. 'That was all that warned you. An icicle saved the world!'

'Yes, an icicle . . . just when I thought I was getting near the beginnings of starting to see a way which might have led to a solution in outline . . . It was vexing. But there's nothing to fear. Their anger has had a long time to cool. My children will not remember their petty rivalries.'

'But they *do* remember,' urged Peter. 'Haven't you looked? Can't you see?'

'Look? See?' The pale face drew back, and swirled through the cave in billows of blackness. 'I am Night: deep, deep Night, who gave the world its being. I have no need to look. I think, and I know. I know everything. Everything!'

'Except the Truth,' Elsa reminded her. 'And you don't know what's happening outside here, right now. They're fighting.'

'You're their *mother*!' Peter rebuked her. 'Don't you know what they're like? They'll destroy the world! You've got to stop *thinking*, and save it!'

'If there's anything left of it to save,' added Moke, squatting on the stone.

A faint tremor shook the rock, and the Mother of All glanced up in quick surprise. Peter listened. There was a dull, muffled ringing in the air, the sign of terrible earthquakes and typhoons in the world beyond. The pale face of the Mother of All once more flitted through the cave, disturbed.

'Fighting . . . ' she murmured. 'All four?'

'All but Holla. She hasn't come—yet. She tried to resist. Send them back! You must!'

The bright face flashed. 'No! And lose my search? Never! The toil of all ages, thrown away? No!'

'But the world will end!'

'It won't. They won't fight. I'll go out to them—call to them. They'll hear me: they'll listen. They'll come. They will. They must!'

'Come back!' Peter shouted. But the black shape had whirled up and away, out through the mouth of the cave, leaving them alone in the dark.

15
Truth

Peter and Elsa ran out of the cave. Before them was a heaving sea of ice, grinding and splintering in the earthquake. All along the edge of the glacier pinnacles of ice were crashing down, and the sky beyond glared with fire. There was no way back. Peter felt sick with anger and despair. The Mother of All had gone, and they were trapped.

Elsa sighed, turned back inside the cave and slumped down next to Moke, who was whistling dismally with a sound like the wind blowing through reeds. Peter stared at her.

'What are you doing?'

'I'm imitating Moke just for once. We tried, and now she's gone and we're stuck. So I'm just going to sit quietly like the goblin here, and see what happens.'

She reached into her bag and got out the roll of birchbark that Grandfather had given her, dipped her pen in the little pot of ink, and began to write.

Moke stopped whistling. 'What's *that*?'

'It's a book. You write in it.'

Moke grunted, and went back to his whistling.

'The . . . end of . . . the world,' Elsa murmured, and then sucked her pen. 'In as few words as possible.'

'Elsa!' Peter burst out. 'You're just going to sit there while the world ends, and write it all down?'

Elsa glared at him. 'What am I supposed to do instead?'

'Well . . . think!'

'You sound like Grandfather.' She went back to her scroll, and then she let out a snort. 'Good grief! It says here, "Note: only milk the nannies." He must have written it in the wrong place. He'll never remember.'

'Don't you understand?' Peter shouted. 'Soon there'll be no nannies, no milking, no questions, no answers, nothing!'

He stared at her a moment more, then turned and stamped out of the cave. Bracing himself against the gale, he picked his way over the shuddering ground until he stood at the very top of the crag. The sight he saw from there was terrible. All round him the ice creaked and groaned, flexing itself like some great armoured creature stirring in its sleep. The whole sky was roaring. Giant figures fought among tatters of cloud, mingled with darkness and fire, lightning and stones, hail and snow; and in between the shifting colours flew the great black shape of Night, Mother of All, circling and darting among the fighters.

As Peter watched, the great thundercloud of Hagal lowered itself over the plain. With a mighty rumble, the hill below reared up like a mountainous giant and came crashing through the clouds, scattering them in fragments, and whirling earth and fire up through the air. Peter's stomach sank with fear. The elements were blending: the world was turning back to chaos, back to the way it had been before the Mother gave it life. First here, then everywhere, all things would be gathered and mixed into a single empty nothingness.

He closed his eyes. But the horror was still there, in the screaming of the wind and the growling of the earth. He opened them again, and saw a dark shape growing out of the clouds and whirling towards him: Mother Night, flying like a cloak carried on the wind. Peter turned and stumbled down the hillside, slipping and falling on the trembling rock. He reached the mouth of the cave just as the Mother of All swept inside and settled over her throne in a swirl of night, her face weeping with rage. Elsa looked up from her writing.

'Well? Did they listen?'

'My search!' wept the Mother of All. 'My search of a thousand thousand years! Lost and gone!'

'Send them back!' yelled Peter. But the weeping face did not look up. He tried to control himself. He had to stay calm, and think. 'Listen,' he said. 'They won't come. They can't. They're too different. If you gather them together, they can only fight. Send them away! Please!'

'My last chance . . . gone! The Truth . . . lost!'

'But the world will end!'

The bright, angry face suddenly looked up. 'Let it end. Never to know . . . to sit in the dark, alone, forever, and never grasp Truth . . .'

Peter turned away, defeated. He glanced at Elsa, who was still sitting and waiting. An idea was beginning to form in his mind. It felt like a dangerous one, but there were no others left to try.

'Listen to me,' he called out, turning back to the throne. 'I don't believe the Truth exists.'

The pale despairing face gazed into his. She looked angry, curious, amazed; and even Elsa was staring at him strangely.

'What did you say?' whispered the Mother of All.

'I mean,' Peter went on solidly, 'what makes you think there *is* such a thing, if you've never found it?'

'There must be,' the face snapped.

'You can't not believe in Truth,' Elsa reproved him. 'What about Grandfather?'

'I think your grandfather's wise the way he is,' Peter replied. 'Lots of people are. There's the voice of the sea, and the shapes in the fire, and Geraia's got her armies of the elements, higher and higher, rose the Mother of All. The burning clouds tinged her face with fire, like the moon rising through mist; and darkness spread in her wake. Now the towering shape straddled the mountain, taller than Brand, darker than the thundercloud, older than all the world.

Dark arms rose from the tower of blackness, and fingers of Night stretched out north and south, east and west and everywhere between, up through the sky and down to the roots of the earth. And then from every one of her fingers there came a stream of movement. Clouds drifted together, gathering first in slender wisps, then larger strands, and finally rolling off across the sky away from the field of battle, this way and that, back to their endless, wandering exile.

Then once more the mountain trembled, and gaping pits yawned for the folk of Fire and Earth. Thrones and minions, armies and courtiers; metal, mineral, and stone; fire and ash and flames, all were sucked back under the earth. Sparks gathered in trains; Brand sank and vanished. And, with a last rumble of troll-drums, the telkins and gettles, boggles and worms and Geraia herself on her throne of gold were all swallowed below ground.

Silence fell. For a moment, Night sat over the mountains, starless, deeper than any night since the world was born. Then the blackness gathered itself up like smoke and vanished back into its home.

A wind sprang up, and Elsa, Peter, and Moke were standing on a crag of rock in a sea of ice, on the mountain on top of the world.

16

The Last Book

It was a long, weary walk down off the mountain. Peter and Elsa were silent and tired, and Moke grumbled continuously. The clouds were gone; a brilliant sun shone down on the winding snowfields and grey slopes of scree.

'I'm going to melt,' Moke warned. 'In a few minutes I'll just be a sad little puddle. Then you'll be sorry.'

But after a while a drizzling bank of mist closed round them, and Moke began sniffing with satisfaction, soaking up the rain as if it were food and drink.

'Drat that goblin,' muttered Elsa. 'I think he *attracts* cold and fog.'

Then suddenly they all stopped. A voice was calling from the mist.

'Moke! Moke!'

A pair of ghostly white faces loomed towards them.

'It's Clatter! And Slodkin!' Moke ran forward, then stopped. 'But I'm not counting snowflakes. It's no good. I won't do it.'

'Never mind that,' came the voice. 'The fleet's a wreck. There's lots of vacancies, and they're looking for a good pilot for a whirlwind. A complete maniac, they said. I told them I knew just the goblin. Well?'

Moke took a few more trembling steps forward, and the mist began to hide him. 'A . . . a whirlwind? Of my very own?'

Now the rain blew across, and his blurred shape faded slowly into the fog. They heard his voice one more time.

underground wisdom, and Hagal has the wisdom of the stars. All those are kinds of wisdom. But you can't gather them together and call them Truth, just like you can't gather the creatures, and hope they'll be friends.'

'Fire burns,' Elsa murmured reflectively. 'Water quenches. Harmony in strife . . . those are things Grandfather's said. I wonder if *he* ever doubted.'

Peter stared at the shimmering face of Night, his heart pounding, waiting for her burst of rage. And meanwhile only the trembling of the ground and the distant roar of the battle broke the silence. Then a long sigh burst from the great, sad face.

'There is no Truth,' she whispered. 'For centuries I've known it at heart. It was the one thought I kept always out of sight, hidden behind others.' She rose from her throne. 'So . . . a world without Truth, empty at its core . . . And I made it!'

Her face twisted with rage, and she darted angrily through the cave, spitting words. 'An empty world! Chaos changed, for nothing! Disorder driven off, and only emptiness gained! The shame! The folly and the waste!' She swept in front of them and hovered, a dark mass of night with its moon-face part-hidden in swirls of shadow.

'I'll destroy it!' she raged. 'Let the whole vain, empty world die!'

'No!' Peter shouted. 'It *isn't* empty. It's got all sorts of creatures and people and things in it—'

'Trees,' Elsa supplied. 'Rivers. Mountains, seas, towns.'

The Mother of All stared at them.

'You've forgotten!' shouted Peter. 'In all those ages of piling thoughts up and pulling them down, you've forgotten the world!'

'Trees . . . ' the Mother of All whispered.

'They've got leaves,' Elsa went on. 'And in the autumn they turn all different colours. Don't you remember?'

The Mother of All was gazing past them into the darkness of the cave. 'Colours . . .'

'There's red,' Elsa prompted her. 'That's sort of loud, and shouts, and green's more quiet . . .'

'This is a terrible thing,' the face whispered. 'I've forgotten . . . forgotten . . .'

'It's not surprising,' Peter said. 'Your mind may be enormous, but it was bound to fill up in the end. All those ages you were searching, and you've lost the truth that you had.'

The face was weeping again now, flitting through the cave like rain in the night.

'And really it's not so terrible,' Peter added. 'The world *is* truth. And it's all still there, trees and animals and clouds and the sea—even boggles and goblins and trolls. It's all out there, waiting for you to see—to see it afresh, as if it had just been made.'

'See . . .' whispered the Mother of All. 'And I'll send my soul through the universe, just as I did at the beginning of all things, when the world was new . . .'

'Then save it first,' Peter urged. 'Send everything back where it belongs.'

'And quickly,' Elsa added. 'It may already be too late.'

The Mother of All gazed at them for a last, long moment, and she seemed to look deep through them, as if she could see the whole world beyond, tottering to its ruin. Then she rose like a column of smoke, and whirled away out of the cave.

Peter, Elsa, and Moke ran outside and up to the top of the crag, stumbling over the twitching, shuddering ground. The din of the earthquake was almost deafening now, and the air was pierced with violent flashes as lightning twined with fire. But above all the warring

'I . . . I'll be back! I'll see you again! You were always good to me,' Moke gulped. 'You took me to nice, cold places . . .'

'Just *don't* come in your whirlwind,' called Peter back. 'I couldn't survive many more of your crashes!'

Moke vanished. A white shape shot up through the mist, and Peter watched as it whisked up and away, back into the clouds. Then the rain stopped and the fog blew apart, and he and Elsa were left alone in bright sun, walking down the newly-washed path.

It was almost night by the time they reached the lip of the last valley and saw the wandering stream below them, with the great boulder set in its middle which hid the house of Grandfather. They hurried down the slope and jumped the water to the steps in the rock, and then they were inside, and there was Grandfather. He did not look at all surprised to see them, and merely asked them to investigate a thing which he proudly claimed to have invented, and which he said was called 'stew'.

Elsa and Peter told him all the story of what had happened on the top of the world, and Grandfather listened in silence. Then, over breakfast next morning, his eyebrows suddenly shot up, and he began to talk.

'Mother Night,' exclaimed Grandfather. 'So she too, was a seeker after Truth, and it was for that reason that she issued her Summons . . . I confess I suspected that something of the sort might be happening. In fact,' he said, glinting at them from under his eyebrows, 'I had rather *hoped*, Granddaughter, that you might come home and tell me the Truth.'

He sighed.

'And the thing which is most crushing of all,' Grandfather went on, 'is that the Mother of All did not even bother to summon mankind: which only shows how little faith she has in our wisdom.'

'What'll you do now, Grandfather?' Elsa asked.

'Now? Now I too must give up my search. It's time I had a break from thinking, and did some seeing instead. I must travel the world, Granddaughter. Truth is everywhere. I can never see it all, perhaps, but if I start right away I can see as much of it as possible. And perhaps I shall make a map—a new sort, that shows things the way they actually are. Yes, I must start at once.'

Elsa stood up. 'And I'll go with you. You'll need someone along to see to the practical side of things.' She began loading her bag with food. Then she looked at Peter, and paused. 'And what about you? Do *you* fancy seeing the world, too?'

Peter shook his head. 'I've seen enough of it for the moment. I'm like the Seafolk, and the storm creatures, and all the rest. Everything has its place, and mine's at home, back on the Island.'

Elsa nodded. 'Well, I expect we'll drop in on you some time. Grandfather'll need to see your island along with everywhere else, won't he?'

Grandfather meanwhile had been scratching away on a final scrap of bark, and now he put down his pen and looked up.

'And Elsa, while you are on your feet—'

'Yes, Grandfather?'

'I have a last book to go in the library.'

He handed her the piece of bark. Elsa looked at it, and read out: *'The Book of Truth'*. She glanced at Grandfather, then back at the scroll. She read, ' "The Truth is many and various." That's it? The whole book?'

'It is, indeed, one of my shorter ones.'

'Where do you want me to put it? In the middle?'

Grandfather smiled. 'No, Elsa. This *isn't* the truth. It only says what the truth is *like*. It's an answer, of a kind— perhaps the most important. No, Granddaughter, leave the middle empty, and put it with the Books of Answers. That way it won't be too easy to find.'

Elsa disappeared down the trapdoor into the library, and when she came back the three of them set off together down the mountain. Peter gazed round at the cliffs and the forests and waterfalls, which looked newly remade in the bright sunshine. These strange, foreign things had come to seem familiar; but still he wanted to fix them all in his mind, so that when he was home on the Island he could call them back whenever he chose, and spin them into the story he was already preparing for Kari, Lotta, and his parents.

Then they came round the last bend of the valley. Below them was the sea, butter-smooth as before, mirroring the green of the land. Peter let out a shout. Down in the bay was the Ship of Stones, waiting for them at anchor, and he could see the crew of Seafolk moving over the deck, blue-white like the wide, open sea, far from the Mainland. As he watched, the anchor was weighed and the sail filled, and the Ship glided towards them.

'*That's* a fine way to start your adventures,' Elsa commented.

But Peter knew the Ship would carry him home.

Other books by Weem Whitaker

The Bold Enchanter
ISBN 0 19 271759 6

'Ah, my dear,' answered the Enchanter with a thin smile, 'dreams can be very deceptive, you know.'

The Bold Enchanter is the one behind all the mischief. When the spells on Earth go wrong, and the wrong kind of magic is unleashed, Tom and Eleanor are the only ones who can save the kingdom. The Queen's wish for Magic and Mystery brought much more than she bargained for, and now someone has to sort it out. But that means many adventures and, somehow, Tom and Eleanor have to find their way to the moon.

The moon, of course, really is made of cheese—Edam, Stilton, every kind of cheese that you can think of. They have to cross the moon cheesescape of boiling Fondue and craggy Cheddar to face the Bold Enchanter in his own castle. Will they win? And what will it all be like when they get home again?

Seeking the Worm
ISBN 0 19 275069 0

The Prince is dead and the Worm has won. And that's how their story book ends. So Charlotte and David decide to change it.

With the help of a magical old alchemy set, they jump right into the book—and into terrible danger.

Will they survive in this unknown world? And can they defeat the evil Worm?

'a cracking adventure.'
                    Times Educational Supplement

'full of colour and imagination.'
                    The Times

Other Oxford fiction

A Handful of Magic
Stephen Elboz
ISBN 0 19 271836 3

Kit, son of the Queen's witch doctor, takes his best friend, Prince Henry, on a night time adventure to see the werewolves at the Tower of London. But when Henry falls into the den and is bitten, it causes a rift between the Queen and Kit's father. The Queen sends for Stafford Sparks, the Royal Superintendent of Scientific Progress, to cure Henry, declaring that magic is dead and that electricity is the power of the future.

Kit is sent to live with his Aunt Pearl in her weird home on the tower of St Paul's cathedral, but he is determined to save Henry from the clutches of Stafford Sparks and his electric shock treatment and prove that magic is still alive. But Kit's attempts to help his friend lead him into terrible danger in the tunnels under London, danger which even magic may not be able to overcome.

Ghost at the Window
Margaret McAllister
ISBN 0 19 271847 9

Ninian House was weird, everyone said so. Built on a rock on the edge of Loch Treen and hundreds of years old, it never seemed to know which century it was in.

When Ewan and his parents moved there, they got used to the house slipping in and out of different periods of history. One minute it would be Victorian, with heavy dark furniture, and the next medieval, with the smell of woodsmoke and sheep. The people they saw from these times never took any notice of them—until one day Elspeth appeared, pleading for Ewan's help. But what could Ewan do to help a ghost from the past? And what was it about the locked cupboard in his bedroom that seemed to terrify her?

The Dalemark Quartet
Diana Wynne Jones

Cart and Cwidder
ISBN 0 19 271832 0

Clennen and his family earn their living as musicians, travelling the lanes of Dalemark in their colourful cart. With warring earls and spies all around, few people move between the North and the South, so they often carry news, and sometimes a passenger.

One such passenger is Kialan. But who is he? And is there any connection between him and the sudden violence that overtakes them on their travels? As Moril tries to discover the mysterious powers of the cwidder it seems as though the fate of his family is somehow tied to Kialan as they become bound together in terror, flight, and music.

Drowned Ammet
ISBN 0 19 271833 9

The people of Holand are bitterly crushed by their tyrannical ruler, whose armies of spies, informers, secret police, and cruel rent collectors terrorize the countryside.

Mitt has grown up with the idea of joining the Freedom Fighters and avenging the wrongs done to his father. But when his part in the plot to kill the wicked ruler goes wildly wrong, he finds himself on the run—and the only place to hide is in the midst of his enemies.

The Spellcoats
ISBN 0 19 271834 7

When her father is killed whilst at war with the Heathens, Tanaqui and her brothers and sister are left to fend for themselves. But the people in their village quickly become suspicious of their Heathen looks and godless ways and soon they are forced to leave.

As they begin a terrifying journey down to the sea Tanaqui realizes the important part she has to play against the evil Kankredin, who is bent on destruction and waiting for them at their journey's end . . .

The Crown of Dalemark
ISBN 0 19 271835 5

For Mitt, North Dalemark seems just as full of spies and tyrants as the South, and it's not long before he himself is blackmailed into carrying out a murder. The intended victim is Noreth, a young girl who has proclaimed herself the rightful heir to the crown of Dalemark.

Soon Mitt and a small band of followers set off with Noreth on a journey to ride the royal road, collect the Adon's gifts, and claim the crown. But all the time they are unaware that the evil forces of Kankredin are among them . . .

A Pattern of Roses
K. M. Peyton
ISBN 0 19 2750615

'T.R.I. 17 February, 1910' was written under one of the drawings found at Inskips, the old cottage which formed part of the Ingram family's new home in the Essex countryside. The initials—the same as his own—intrigued Tim Ingram, and his curiosity was aroused further by the discovery of a mossy headstone in the village churchyard which revealed that 'T.R.I.'—Tom Inskip—had died one month short of his sixteenth birthday. Tim decides to try and unravel the mystery of Tom's early death, but the deeper he delves into the past, the more Tom Inskip seems to come to life. Is he sending a message—or is it a warning . . .

A Store of Secrets
Stephen Elboz
ISBN 0 19 275067 4

Bridie's grandfather has vanished, and the menacing Crickbone brothers have taken over his yard. Suddenly Bridie finds herself all alone in the city. It never looked so strange and threatening before. But then she begins to discover friends in the unlikeliest of places, and ends up meeting Miss Firbanks, owner of the Byzantium Bazaar, a department store where time stands still and dust covers everything.

Now all Bridie has to do is solve the mystery of what happened to Gramps, and for that she enlists the help of the street people.